"THAT MAN IS A VAMPIRE."

At the turn of the 20th century, thousands of poor Japanese girls were tricked or kidnapped by *zegen* - Japanese "impresarios". They were smuggled on steamships and sent to Singapore, where they were sold for sex to a largely male population while the British authorities struggled to contain prostitution and disease.

In 1906, a young magistrate in Nagasaki meets the son of a prostitute, who tells him an incredible story of human trafficking. The two men recruit Sparrow, an American woman boxer and stowaway, who had no money and was "basically game for anything". The three friends hide themselves on board the luxury steamship the *Tobi Maru* bound for Singapore, in pursuit of the greatest *zegen* of all, the legendary Oguri.

スタジオウェナ

All Text © 2017 Wena Poon
Cover Design, Interior Design, and
Interior Photography © 2017 Wena Poon
Front and Back Cover Photography © 2017 Wena Poon
All rights reserved.
A スタジオウェナ Production
Austin, Texas, USA
www.wenapoon.com
ISBN-13: 978-1976030420
ISBN-10: 1976030420

Front cover: The *Hikawa Maru*, Yokohama, Japan
(Kobe-Seattle, 1929)
Back cover: Vintage silk kimono

THE
GREAT
IMPRESARIO
OGURI

方慧娜 著

WENA POON

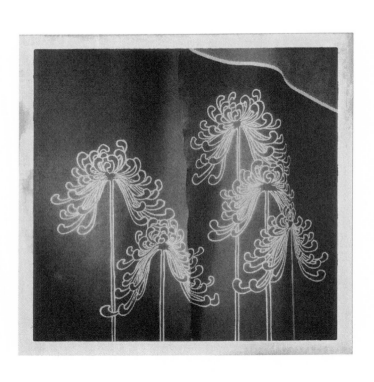

女衒小栗

スタジオウェナ

SCENES

THE BOXER

They said that when the fighting started, the local magistrate Nakayama was the only person in the entire pub who did not turn around. Not only did he remain seated the whole time, with his back to the melée, he calmly ordered "Darjeeling Tea", which stumped the pub owner. Who ever heard of a customer ordering *any* kind of tea in a sailor's pub in Nagasaki? He had to send a boy to make a special purchase.

When the person who started the fight was brought, bloodied and bruised, to kneel before Nakayama, the pub owner said only one Japanese word issued forth from the magistrate's lips: "*Kanpeki.*" Perfect. Perfect? What's so perfect about a ten minute brawl that cost hundreds of dollars' worth of damage? cried the pub owner in dismay, bitterly demanding reparations.

Frriiip! A hand shot up in front of the pub owner's face. It dangled a beautiful gold watch.

"This," said Nakayama. "Is a Jess Hans Martens pocket watch. My father ordered it when I was born in 1881. It was shipped from Germany – do not ask me to name the town because I cannot pronounce it."

"Oh!" cried the pub owner in delight. "I accept!" He reached for it, but it disappeared back into the magistrate's vest pocket.

"You may have the chain, which should be sufficient to repair this place," said the young man, unclipping the gold chain and pooling it in the pub owner's outstretched palm. Then he turned to his prisoner. "Now. What's this all about?"

The prisoner said nothing. He tried to get up. The two policemen forced him to kneel again.

An audience had already formed. More people streamed in gleefully from the street. It was dinner time: with luck they'd get some theater to go with it.

"Well?" Nakayama repeated his previous question in Dutch, then French, then Russian. All to no effect. The prisoner was clearly a Westerner. Having run out of languages he vaguely knew, Nakayama was about to give up when the prisoner said, very clearly in English, "Are you going to let me go or not?"

"Ah. You didn't look like you're from England," said Nakayama in English.

"I'm not from England, I'm American, you idiot."

He was relieved. It would have been worrying, for example, if he had to proceed further in Russian – he would have to send for the interpreter from the courthouse. He would lose face very badly in front of the expectant crowd: he, the newly-installed magistrate, painfully under-aged (he could not grow a moustache), under-tall (despite his Western suit) and supremely under-qualified (according to the local press). But having been born and raised in London, Nakayama had no difficulty lashing out in English. "And you're female! What the devil are you doing in men's clothes and fighting?"

"We weren't fighting, we were in a boxing match."

"In the middle of a dining establishment?"

"It was spontaneous."

"And the victor?"

"Myself, clearly, since he ran away the moment your policemen appeared." She spat. Quite convincingly. From her appearance he could tell she lacked food, money, sleep and friends. Unusual. All Western women he had ever dealt with since he arrived in Nagasaki were wealthy expatriate wives at luncheons or the occasional prostitute in court. She belonged to neither category. A stowaway? She was in Manchu dress.

"So you beat him?" said Nakayama. The pub owner finally brought him a steaming mug of "*da jirin*" tea. He sniffed, but did not drink. He set the cup down. "And was there a prize?"

She nodded. "Ten dollars. But his friends had bet the money. They've disappeared with him. No thanks to you."

Nakayama beckoned to his policemen and conferred with them. They bowed curtly and disappeared. He pulled a handkerchief from his breast pocket and handed it to her. "Clean up. I know who those three Chinese are. They'll be brought in shortly. We'll finish the boxing match outside, by the dockyard. We have to make it quick. I need to be home in time for dinner with my mother."

The crowd burst into excited chatter.

The prisoner got up and cleaned her face. She retied her hair. Someone offered her his beer, which she drank quickly. Nakayama put on his top hat and picked up his cane. The crowd stuck close to his heels.

"Where are you going?" cried the prisoner.

"The dockyard, of course. Right outside. I expect to see you there shortly. Please do not try to escape. The winner shall receive one hundred dollars, furnished by me. The loser shall get jail time for disturbance of the peace." He tipped his hat at her and disappeared into the crowd.

It is a sweltering August. The year? 1906.

✳

"But I won," said the prisoner to the local magistrate.

"Indeed. And I paid you," said Nakayama.

"Why am I still in jail?"

"This isn't *really* jail, it just happens to be where I work," he said patronizingly, pushing open a swing door. "Like it? It's a brand new building, modeled after a courthouse in Germany. After you."

She entered a dark corridor. A yellow bar of late afternoon sun came in through a high window. Otherwise the basement of the courthouse was cool and desolate. It smelled of new brick and whitewash. Her footsteps echoed.

"Notice the new design of steel bars in the cells," said Nakayama proudly. He rapped them with his walking stick: *clank clank*. "Look, iron grates on the floor; windows to let out hot air at the top. The old building did not ventilate well. Air circulation: so critical. The winters are mild enough; it's the summer humidity that I worry about."

She muttered darkly under her breath and refused to meet his gaze.

"I may sound enthusiastic about prison reform, but don't get me wrong. I actually don't believe in the deterrent effect of incarceration," said Nakayama. Ever since he returned to Japan, he had not had the chance to converse in English with many people. He was unusually chatty with his prisoner. It was as if a lid had come off; he looked almost delighted. "I much prefer fines. Prisoners take up space; cash doesn't. We need liquidity. There's so much to fix. More fire equipment, for instance; more health inspectors. So far I've only kept one prisoner here. You have to meet him. Speaks English and Japanese. From Singapore. Really nice kid, even if his mother was a penniless prostitute." He raised his voice. It bounced off the walls, *"Koto-kun genki? Tomodachi da yō!"* (How are you doing Koto? I've brought you a friend!)

Nakayama unlocked the last cell. *Clannk!*

The prisoner snapped, "I can't believe you're putting me in jail! I knew it! This town's as crooked as they say!"

"I'm not putting you in jail," said Nakayama haughtily. "We're simply having A Meeting."

His prisoner expelled a sound of contempt.

He continued, "I would much prefer to have the Meeting in my house, of course, but it's Wednesday, which is when my mother visits. She'd never come *here*. Ah, Koto, meet – what's your name again, woman?"

"Sparrow."

The shabby boy in the corner rose. He was incredibly pale, tall and thin, with ruddy cheeks and cheekbones that stood out a mile on either side. He rubbed his right hand against his shirt and offered to shake hands. Too late, he noticed that her fingers were bruised and her knuckles bleeding. He let go of her hand hastily. "Koto. Who're you?"

"What kind of name is Koto?" she exclaimed.

"What kind of name is Sparrow?" he shot back.

"I beg your pardon, it is my real name!" she said. "My family name."

The magistrate firmly separated the two. "Now that you have been properly introduced, let me explain to you the nature of the Mission."

The two turned to him, aghast. "*Mission?*"

DARJEELING TEA

"Goodness, what kept you?" said his mother in astonishment. "I have much to discuss."

Nakayama let the maid help him shrug off his suit jacket. It was too warm for humid Nagasaki summers. At home he need not keep up appearances. He went into a little side room to change into comfortable Japanese dress. "How have you been, dear Mother?" he called, tying his *yukata* belt. "How is the countryside?"

"*Much* cooler than being in the city. The other day, we heard that some foreigners tried to move into our neighborhood."

"Oh dear."

"So we hid all the horses and told them there were no transportation options into the city. They looked around and left. Thank God!"

"Country life is so exciting," came Nakayama's voice. It was hard to tell if he was being sarcastic.

She fanned herself with a paper fan. From time to time she folded it and brandished it like a stick for emphasis. "If they try to rent a house, I'll swoop in and rent it first so they can't have it. It's the only neighborhood left that they haven't invaded." She pointed the fan at the wall, even though he wasn't in the room. "And what's that cross doing on the wall? I forbid you to convert to Catholicism!"

"It's only to fend off vampires," came the placid reply.

"Good! You are not allowed to adopt foreign religion."

"*Hai, hai.* I'm starving."

"I made your favorite."

The Nakayama townhouse was built in the 1870s. It had been furnished Western-style, as dictated by his Eurocentric father and grandfather. Only the kitchen remained Japanese: the wives and servants had insisted upon it. When Nakayama sat down at the European, baroque-looking dinner table, he found a dozen photographs neatly arranged around his place setting.

"You need to choose," said his mother fervently. "It's driving me mad. I can't decide."

He picked a photograph and held it up. "I think this one would suit you rather well. Order it in green?"

"Green? No, not the *dress!* The *girl!* Pick the girl for me to interview to be your future bride!"

"Oh, that again," said Nakayama, setting down the photograph. He looked at all of the photographs, carefully this time. Twelve Japanese young women in the height of Western fashion, their hair combed into huge balloons. Half of them posed with lacy umbrellas. They were otherwise indistinguishable from each other.

The maid served them each a savory soufflé. He looked at the yellow soufflé admiringly, then patted it gently with a spoon. It wobbled. "I want to get married when I'm forty."

"Pooh! Forty!"

"That would give me enough time to cultivate the world's biggest whiskers, which would just have begun to turn slightly silver. I would then look incomparably dashing with one of these young ladies at my elbow, don't you think? Fifteen more years, Mother."

She shuddered. "Stop it! I can't wait that long."

"Are you ill?"

"No? What are you talking about?"

"I would hurry if I knew you were ill, but you'd have to be – incontrovertibly – at death's door," said Nakayama. He broke a hole in the soufflé with his spoon. A bunch of steam escaped. "I would miss you, of course, on Wednesdays. A wife would soften the blow. And make the soufflés."

"Please do not talk about your mother's death. When a woman crosses the threshold of fifty, she gets very sensitive about such things."

"I can't help it, Mother. The only time I would replace you with a wife is when you are really gone. I only have room for a single female in my life: any more would upset my constitution, not to mention my schedule. It's bad enough that we live next door to a little girl who practices piano eight hours a day. It makes me so furious when she makes a mistake, because she starts all over again from the top! I mean, *Rondo alla Turca*, of all things. It *already* repeats." He paused and gestured despairingly.

They listened.

He said, "Didn't Mozart go insane?"

"*Gaman*, dear. *Gaman*." (Tolerate!)

He shuddered. "So please stop wishing for me to get a replacement soufflé-maker. Why that would be tantamount to wishing yourself dead."

His mother rested her cheek on her hand. "I see that coming home to Japan has done you little good, Sen-*chan*."

"It's done me *heaps* of good. Why, I have a proper job now. I am a man with a mission."

"The newspapers say your jail cells are empty. Why aren't you out catching crooks?"

"I *am* catching crooks. I can't do it openly as my life would be in danger. And *yours* as well. With Father abroad, we are but little hens at the mercy of the fox, dear Mother."

"Oh?" She lowered her voice and darted a glance at the door. "Are you on to something big?"

"No. Not really. I spend my afternoons pushing paper around, ordering new toilets for my building. I just have to do this for two years and I'll be promoted to Tokyo. I've developed a satisfactory routine. At precisely four o'clock every afternoon, I take two policemen with me for my daily patrol. It's good exercise, and excellent for public relations. The shopping's better in London, but I have found one or two – "

His mother erupted in impatience. "I do wish you would do something about the foreign gangsters!"

"Actually, the most serious crimes are committed by domestic gangs. However, we have chosen to overlook them because they bribe government officials."

"I refuse to believe you. It is always the foreigners that commit crimes. In broad daylight!"

"What's done in broad daylight is less injurious to the Nation's health than what's done in the dark."

"But look at what the Chinese are doing!"

He narrowed his eyes. "You want me to take on *the Chinese?*"

"Well, yes," she said lamely. "Your father would be pleased if you made a difference in this town."

"If I take on the Chinese, you'd be having to find another husband for these girls before Christmas." He swept up the photographs in a neat pile and shuffled them like a deck of cards. "And remember, Mother. If there is any of my body left: cremated, *not* buried in Catholic cemetery please. I hate earthworms."

"Stop being morbid. I'm eating."

She refreshed his tea. Once again, the faint sounds of a child practicing piano.

"She *is* getting better each time I visit," said his mother hopefully.

"How can she not?" said Nakayama darkly. "She has no other life! If she must play, why can't she play something more modern – something with pentatonic scales, for example? I wonder if she takes requests."

"How I wish you stuck to piano!" She went on to enumerate his other childhood flaws, each of which was extremely unimportant yet very dear to her heart.

"Look, *kaa-san*!" Nakayama pushed his plate across the table. He had managed to eat all of the inside of the puffy soufflé, leaving a deflated exterior.

"And you still play with your food," concluded his mother sadly.

"I have to do these things," said Nakayama, ringing for the maid. "Otherwise you'd have nothing to complain about in your letters to Father. Would you like some sake? I found an excellent local brewery. Really good value, too."

✳

"What the hell are these photographs?" said Sparrow.

"They're Japanese girls who wish to get married," said Koto. "Perhaps he wants you to marry them?" He examined two giant, cloth-wrapped bundles that the policemen had deposited in their jail cell. They each contained a futon, a tiny pillow filled with some kind of grain, and a beautifully soft duvet stuffed with pure, finely-spun silk fibers, which were the best and most expensive kind of filling. This was because Nakayama's mother came from a silk-making family, and these were duvets his relatives had sent to him as gifts (which he had never touched). Everything smelled of dried lavender. And there were socks, slippers, and a *nemaki*, a thin cotton sleeping robe for each of them.

"*You* marry them," Sparrow flicked the photos at Koto.

He ducked. "The photos were in *your* bundle! Hee hee hee!"

There was a note.

Dear Sparrow, can you pick which dress you wish to wear on board the Tobi Maru? I've already decided on Koto's disguise (he doesn't get to choose). However, as I know nothing about women's Fashions, I have no choice but to ask you to please let Kiku (the shorter policeman) know your choice and he will go to the tailor shop and have it made in time for your sailing. You simply cannot be an American tourist and go on board wearing your Manchu men's clothing, you would spoil everything. More tomorrow. Good night.

Sincerely, Nakayama Sen 中山 暹

Sparrow looked up. Koto had already assembled his futon. He put on his *nemaki*. "This has got to be the most luxurious jail cell ever," he said. "It's my first time in prison, what about you? Man. All other jails are gonna stink after this first experience." He leapt into bed and stretched out blissfully. His legs were so long that they stuck out on the other side. "All that's missing is a wonderful hot bath."

"What if I just say no to the mission?"

"Eh?" He opened one eye.

"You signed up for it. *I* didn't. It's *your* mission, really. Oguri is your enemy and Nakayama's obsession. Not my problem." She unrolled her bedding. "My parents are gone. I'm free as a bird. I don't need you or Nakayama."

"Don't you want to see Oguri in jail? After everything I told you?"

"I don't care either way. He's Japan's problem, not mine."

"Don't you want to help rescue those women?"

"I just want to box, and get better at boxing."

"That's all you care about?"

"That's right."

"Boxing?"

"That's right."

"Don't you have any higher purpose in life?"

"Not really. Do you?"

Koto considered, yawning. "When I find my sister, I'm gonna take her back to Amakusa to my mother's old village. Then I'm gonna buy us a fishing boat. And I'm gonna catch fish and oysters and crabs and things, and we'll just live off that."

Sparrow flopped on to her futon. "God, how old are you?"

"Nineteen. So?"

"You act like you're nine. For starters, have you ever been to Amakusa?"

"No."

"From the little I've heard, it's a dump. And how are you going to buy a boat? You'd need serious money for that. If your mother's family had any money, they wouldn't have sold her to sexual slavery in Singapore."

"They didn't sell her!" protested Koto. "She volunteered. They were starving. She was the oldest daughter and she volunteered to work overseas to support her family and to serve the Emperor. That's what she told me anyway. Before she died."

"And you believe her."

Koto blew his long and untidy bangs. They fluttered up and down. "She thought she was being recruited to work overseas as a maid. That's what Oguri the *zegen* tells everybody. She didn't know."

"*Zegen*. Is that what you guys call pimp?"

"In Japanese it is."

"How do you write it? In Chinese characters?"

Koto had been adopted and raised by a respectable Chinese family in Singapore. He knew his *kanji*. "The first word is the word for *woman*," he sketched in the air.

女

"The second word is a weird archaic word. They never use it anymore except to say *zegen*. Take the word for *travel*, pull it apart, and put the word for *pitch dark* in the middle."

街

He wrote it out several times so she finally understood. Sparrow was born in China, but she had never seen the word for pimp. "Woman," she said thoughtfully. "The word for travel. And sandwiched within, pitch darkness. Like in a ship's hold. What a perfect word for trafficking of girls."

"*Darō*," he agreed. "Doesn't it just give you the heebie jeebies?"

"Well, when we get on that ship, at least I'd be travelling first class, because I'm American. That's what Nakayama promised."

Koto scowled suddenly. "Wait a minute. Do only white people go on first class? Where would I be?"

Sparrow laughed. "Well, you're half Japanese and half − what? Did you ever find out?"

"Some yellow race, obviously." He pointed at his face. "Chinese is most statistically probable. My adopted family is Chinese."

"Perhaps he's dreamed up a Japanese or Chinese persona for you to travel in first class. Worst case scenario, you'll be in Third."

"I'll take Third. Least I'll get a cabin and a bed. I've only travelled Cargo. Last time, I sat between wicker hampers. In a storm they can roll on you and crush you to death. Not to mention the floor. Constantly sticky with vomit and pee and poop."

"There's no toilet in Cargo? Even when I stole on board I went to the toilets."

"You had to go upstairs to the toilets. In Cargo most people were so seasick they couldn't even move. Just lay there and pooped on themselves. After seven days of darkness, they come up to the surface and they say they feel reborn. Third Class would be paradise in comparison! I wonder what First is like." He propped himself up on an elbow. "So you're going then?"

"I haven't decided," she yawned. "It *is* a free first-class trip to Singapore, and that ship sounds like a real luxury liner. All I have to do is to keep my eyes peeled for the missing girls and report when we arrive, right? Seems simple enough. Especially if *you* do all the work. I'll supervise. I'm good at supervising kids."

"Shut up! I'm going no matter what. Even if I have to travel Cargo. I have to find my sister."

Sparrow said sleepily, "How are you ever going to find her? You only have her name, not even a photo."

"Faith."

"Are you Catholic?" she asked.

"Yep. Are you?"

"Hell, no. My parents were missionaries so I'm nothing."

"*So* you're nothing? What a non-sequitur. What were they missionaries of?"

"No idea. Not Catholic. What other options are there?"

"Anglican? Baptist?"

"Something along those lines. Whatever they practice in Virginia. I have no idea. I was born in Tianjin."

"How could you not know what Christian religion your own parents were missionaries of?"

"If they mentioned it, I was so little I didn't know what it meant. They were always out on the road, *missionarizing*. I was left in the care of monks in a Buddhist temple. Supposedly for my own safety: foreigners are always getting lynched. The monks didn't know what to do with me, so they simply raised me along with the orphan boys. We were taught kungfu. For discipline."

"Your parents are Christian and you do not believe in God?"

"I believe in the God of Boxing."

Koto fell silent for a while, then – "If I travel Third Class, I could arrange a boxing match for you. That kind of thing goes on in Third Class. I'll be the *zegen* of boxing." He chuckled. "Gosh, you could win us real money if you're really as good as Nakayama says."

But Sparrow was sound asleep.

He kicked off his duvet. It was too warm. He turned over and buried his face in his bean pillow. He never had a brand new bean pillow before. The beans inside were crisp and smelled wonderfully raw, of the country. What kind of bean was it, he wondered, feeling them through the fabric. Sometimes it was buckwheat, sometimes it was seeds or the dried pits of small fruit. He wondered about Nakayama.

He thought about his biological mother. He got to spend the last few days of her life with her. It was at the brothel owner's insistence, actually – she wanted the dying woman off the premises. So he talked to his pastor who recommended a Catholic hospice. He took her there in a rickshaw, then carried her up the stairs. She weighed nothing by that point.

"*Ne,* Koto-*san,*" she said. It was a high-ceilinged top floor, barn-like, with windows that let in plenty of air. Very different from the brothel. "Truth is, I almost didn't want to give you away." She chuckled.

"*Yappari* (As I thought)," he said, smiling.

"Of course, you won't believe me."

"I believe you. You know why? Because Mother always said so."

"She said that?"

"She was paranoid that you would change your mind. She said she had already gotten ready my cot, my milk bottles. She had bought everything. Then at the very last minute, she had a dream that you changed your mind and refused to give me up. It happens quite often, she said. Especially if the baby is born fat and healthy, without disease. So when she came to the hospital and saw me, she thought she was doomed. I was fair-skinned and smooth and plump, as heavy and perfect as a melon. There is no way you would let go of me once you saw me. So she told the nurse to wrap me up completely, so you could only see a tiny bit of my face, and she took me to you and said, "*Ii no? Ii no?*" (Okay? Okay?) One of the few Japanese words she knew. And you didn't even cast a glance at me, you just gave a nod and said, "*Ii yō.*" (Okay). And with that she hastily carried me off like a thief."

"She told you all that?" His mother was astonished.

"*Sō.*" Koto never stopped smiling. "It is one of our favorite bedtime stories when I was

little. It was my version of *Momotaro*, except
that they didn't find me in a peach." He dipped
the corner of a handkerchief in water and wet
her mouth. She was too weak to get up to
drink.

"How could I go back on my word?" she
said. "If it weren't for your mother, I would be
giving birth under a bridge. She bought me a
bed in a ward. She needn't have worried.
Prostitutes know how to give children away.
Never breastfeed him, we tell each other.
Breastfeed him for a week, and he's yours for
life. Don't look at him, let the nurse take him
away the moment he appears. Never tell the
father. If the father knows and insists on
coming to the hospital to see it, tell him the
baby is diseased, covered with sores, or was
born dead. If the father sees a healthy baby, a
boy, he'd start getting ideas. He'd make
demands. I knew all that. Yet I still looked at
you. I couldn't help myself. I snuck a peek at
you before the nurse took you away to show
your mother. I smelled you. You smelled so
nice." She had loved the father of the baby, to
whom Koto bore a startling resemblance. Of
course, she did not say any of this. It was bad
enough that the boy had found her. "And yes, I
almost changed my mind. But there was only
one life for you in the brothel. It was already
filled with unwanted children. Damaged girls;
broken boys. My son will not be a criminal.

Your parents were educated people. I knew I wouldn't be so lucky again."

She closed her eyes. "They were Chinese. How did you end up with a Japanese name? I'd have thought they wanted to cut off ties."

"Father picked this Chinese character for me, *zheng* 箏," he sketched it in the air, but she shook her head.

"*Dame desu yō*, Koto-*san*," she said sadly. "I can't read or write."

He wished she wouldn't call him Koto-*san*. She was so respectful of him, as if he was a proper gentleman. It made him so sad. "It means 'kite'. At home my name is *Xiao Zheng*. But he told me it has two meanings, it also means the zither." Koto mimed plucking the strings in the air. "In Japanese *zheng* is read as *koto*. Geishas play it."

"Ah, yes. I know what that is," she said tiredly. "I posed with one at the photography studio. Long ago. Of course, I didn't know how to play it. It was all for show."

"Father said I could choose which reading I liked when I grew up. He was a bit of a scholar."

"I see. I was right about them."

"*Sō*." (Yeah) He wanted to add a lot more, to thank her for giving him to them, but he didn't know how to say it without sounding strange. So he just sat and held her hand awkwardly.

"*Ne,* Koto-*san*," she took a deep breath and stared at the ceiling, as if looking at an imaginary point above it. "Don't be a *koto*. In life it's better to be a kite."

ON BOARD THE
TOBI MARU

A few days ago, in a certain unnamed naval dockyard in Nagasaki.

He was a ship chandler. He only spoke to Nakayama Sen on the condition of anonymity, and under the cover of night. He had insisted that Nakayama come alone.

"Are you sure about this?" asked the magistrate.

"One can never be sure of anything," said the chandler. He wore traditional Japanese dress. His back tattoos encircled his neck to end behind his left ear. "The fire was probably an accident. Coal does sometimes spontaneously ignite in the hold of the ship. Their bodies had been completely burned away, so I can't tell you how many girls were in that coal storage bunker. But I know that when I went in to shovel the debris, I found those two things. I stopped shoveling. I'm a superstitious man. I haven't told anyone. But I've heard of your old man's reputation. So I'm risking my life to tell you. I trust you will not reveal your sources. If something happens to me, you will never learn anything in this town again."

"How could I reveal my source," said Nakayama sweetly. "When I don't even know your name?"

The old man grunted. "I knew Oguri when he was a young boy. I used to throw him my scraps. He had nothing. Now he is in European coattails hosting gala balls and bribing officials left and right. Calls himself an impresario. Walks past me and doesn't even recognize me. That's modern life for you. Mind you, I don't blame him. In this society, you stay in the class you're born in forever, unless you're willing to commit crimes." He looked Nakayama up and down. "Not that people like you understand what I mean."

The magistrate wisely chose to say nothing. He reached into his pocket and offered the chandler a small envelope. "I am grateful."

"No thanks," said the old man gruffly.

"It's my personal money," said the magistrate. "Not the Government's."

"Use it to burn some incense for the girls' souls. If you can be bothered."

The chandler shuffled off into the night. Nakayama did not leave right away. He crouched down by the edge of the water. The waves licked at the pier gently, making gurgling noises. Carefully, he unfolded the handkerchief that the chandler had given him. He pulled a book of matches from his pocket.

Shaaaak! The match flared.

A scrap of floral kimono fabric. A white shard of bone.

✳

TEN FINGER SONG

This little sailor wore a turban
This little sailor had none
This little sailor had golden locks
This little sailor was scum

This little sailor locked me up on Tuesday
This little sailor drank and cried
This little sailor made me pregnant
This little sailor gave us rum
This little sailor owed me money
And this little sailor went wee wee wee all the *way home!*

✳

Bifff!
Pam!
Bop!
Crash!

"She's wonderful," whispered the coal trimmer standing next to Koto. "My buddy is the best boxer in Klang, and she's matching him blow for blow."

"What's the best boxer in Klang doing working as a coal trimmer on a ship?" Koto whispered back. They were in the coal storage bunkers below deck, a terribly hot and sweaty place. All fifty-three coal trimmers working on the luxury steamship had paused in their activity (shoveling coal) in order to watch the Malay boxer take on a Western female.

Bifff!
Pam!
Bop!

"He's on the run from the law. It's easy to get a job as a coal trimmer," said the man. "With firemen they're more picky. But think about it – who wants to work in a coal bunker, breathing in this shitty air, with no responsibility other than making sure that the weight of the coal is evenly distributed so that the ship won't list to one side? When they first told me that such a job existed, I laughed."

"So did I," said Koto. He remembered the conversation with Nakayama very well. And bitterly. Sparrow would travel First Class, and Koto? In disguise as a coal trimmer. Part of his disguise entailed him actually having to work as one. It would "help in the investigations."

"I thought I would be feeding coal into the fire," said the coal trimmer. "That would at least be satisfying in some small way. But no, I just move coal about, from port to starboard, from bow to stern. In this noise and heat and semi-darkness. Why you couldn't even recognize your own mother's face under this soot. What a joke. It's like some routine the Hell Judge Yama would think up for Purgatory."

Bifff!

Pam!

Bop!

The Klang boxer shouted something in Malay. His friend hurriedly translated, "Enough!"

Sparrow's face was thoroughly blackened from soot particles adhering to her sweat. "Awesome! Hand over the money."

Everyone began paying up. Koto made a collection round.

"Who's next?" panted Sparrow.

One of the men said in Japanese, which was translated by Koto, that there was apparently a Japanese boxer travelling in Third Class on the way to an exhibition match at a hotel in Singapore. A fellow by the name of Hachibana or Tachibana or something like that.

"Have you ever sparred with a Japanese boxer?" asked Koto worriedly.

"Are you kidding," said Sparrow, spitting soot. "I may be American but I was trained by Chinese monks. My style was *meant* to fight the Japanese. Arrange it."

The men clapped. Sparrow's reputation began to spread on board the *Tobi Maru*.

✳

A country suburb of Nagasaki.

Nakayama's mother wrote a letter to her husband.

... I remember you said that I had spent such a long time crafting the gears of this music box. The spokes have long been polished and set in place: I was

not to worry. All it needed was someone to come and lift the lid. With a click the music would play.

I knew that something would happen when we moved here. I didn't think that it would happen so quickly. It came in the form of a half-Japanese boy from Singapore, a prostitute's son.

The day Sen met Koto, his fate was sealed.
The lid has been lifted.

✳

Bifff!
Pam!
Bop!

The elegant Japanese man in a silk top hat handed his card to Koto.

OGURI JUNICHIRO
IMPRESARIO OF FINE ACTS
NAGASAKI – SHANGHAI – HONG KONG –
SINGAPORE - MANILA – SAN FRANCISCO

He had a giant walrus moustache and was much younger than Koto had ever imagined. Koto was in shock. *Oguri! On this ship! Nakayama never said a thing!*

"I suppose my reputation precedes me," said Oguri grandly.

Koto trembled. "Yes, sir."

"Are you the *zegen* of this English boxer?"

"She's American, sir."

"Even better. I have many American clients. And how did you come about acquiring such a fine specimen of modern entertainment?"

"S-she needed a translator." Koto could not think of anything else to say.

Bifff!

Pam!

Bop!

"Someone like you could never do anything for her," Oguri looked Koto up and down, very slowly and deliberately, all the while twirling the curly end of his giant, shiny moustache. *Do people really do that?* thought Koto, dazed. *Is this guy for real?* He *is the man who sold my mother to a brothel???* He was hyperventilating in sheer panic.

Finally Oguri said, "I will make you a good offer."

Bifff!

Pam!

Bop!

"She's not for sale," mumbled Koto.

CRASH! A roar went up on the third class deck as Sparrow sent Tachibana flying into the crowd.

"Out of the way!"

"Good Lord!"

"Mind the baby!"

As if on cue, all the children began to cry.

A Japanese woman next to Koto shouted, "We're done for! Even our top male athletes are too small to take on Europeans! We can't even beat their women."

"Aye!" her husband agreed.

CRASH! Tachibana was sent reeling into them. "I heard you!" he yelled in Japanese. "It's not about size, it's about speed and agility!"

"Actually, it *is* about size!" she yelled. "Even in sumo!"

"Women! All they care about is size!" he fired back.

Bifff!

Pam!

Bop!

Koto stared at the two boxers. His head swam. He was sure he had seen this diminutive Japanese boxer before. But he could not for the life of him think where. He tried to recall the boxing matches he had watched in Singapore.

Oguri loomed again before him, looking extremely satisfied. "I don't need to stay to watch this," he said. "It's obvious who will win. I'm in Cabin 8 in First Class. Bring her to me when you are ready. You will not regret it." He left in a flutter of silk coattails.

It was a pity that the *zegen* left, for Tachibana unexpectedly made a big comeback. The match went on for quite a few rounds after that, with hardly any rules. The crowd egged them on, with the Japanese roaring for

Tachibana and the Europeans and other races screaming "Spa-rrow! Spa-rrow! Spa-rrow!" And because the Chinese saw her Manchu clothing, they called out, *Jin Que! Jin Que! Jin Que!* (Golden Sparrow, because one had to add gold to anything one admired so terribly).

A few articles of furniture were broken.

Finally the match was called in Sparrow's favor. Tachibana lay face down, unable to get up.

Jin Que Wan Sui! (Hurray for Golden Sparrow!)

Sparrow was hoisted on the shoulders of two burly Chinese men with shaved heads and long braided pigtails. They made a victory lap while people showered her with small change of assorted international currencies.

Koto felt sorry for Tachibana. He peeled him off the floor, dragged him to a quiet corner, and flagged down a waiter. "Have a beer."

"Ah, thanks," said Tachibana, sipping gratefully. He winced. The beer was not to his liking. He offered it back to Koto. "Did we get a positive ID?"

"Eh?" said Koto.

"That fop from First Class who was talking to you. You got his card."

"You know him? That's Oguri Junichiro, the famous impresario."

"Is that what the card said? Show me the card."

Koto pulled it out of his kimono. "Here. You can have it. Though I doubt he would be interested in you. It's my friend he's after."

Tachibana pocketed the card. "And he also said his name to you. As he was presenting you the card?"

"Of course."

"*Kanpeki*." (Perfect).

"Ah!" Koto peered closer, then pushed the boxer's bangs out of his face. "Crap! Did Sparrow not recognize you?"

"Of course she did. Eventually," said Nakayama (for that was who 'Tachibana' was). "As expected, she fought on without batting an eyelid. That woman is a *machine*."

"You look so different in Japanese dress! I could not place your face!"

"A trick I discovered long ago in boarding school. The hair helps."

"It's true, you look so much older when you put wax in it and comb it back."

"That's my 'magistrate' look."

Koto downed the rest of the beer in shock. "What the hell are you doing here?"

"Running away from an arranged marriage." Nakayama got up and limped a little. "Actually, I'm working."

Koto whispered, "Do you have your men on board too?"

"Ten members of the Japanese Maritime Police," said Nakayama, *sotto voce*. "They're working in your department. Coal trimmers are always in short supply, so I was able to fix everyone up in a jiffy, no questions asked."

"Why do you need me if you have ten of them?"

Nakayama winked. "People of Oguri's level can smell a cop a mile off. Only you and Sparrow can get close to him."

"Have you ever met him?"

"Never. He, on the other hand, has undoubtedly seen my official photograph in the papers. I trust he didn't recognize me just now. I deliberately held back until he left. People like him only have eyes for the winner. But I did give old Sparrow a good run for her money, don't you think? Towards the end?"

"You still lost."

"Don't remind me." Nakayama felt his ribs. He would get a magnificent bruise tomorrow. "Still, it was worth it. You managed to get Oguri to identify himself to you. Everybody knows his name, but he no longer goes to public events. As far as we know, he has never had his picture taken. We don't have any official description of him. Those who know would never tell. With his card, and you as a witness, I'm gold."

"You're wasting your time," said Koto glumly. "I haven't seen any evidence of human trafficking on this ship. There's nothing in the coal bunkers except coal. I've shoveled every pile. Unless they've spontaneously combusted, there are no girls being kept down there."

Nakayama felt gingerly in his mouth for any loose teeth. "There is still one place we haven't checked."

"Where?"

Nakayama informed him of a certain compartment located between the boiler rooms. Koto said hurriedly, "I'll go take a look now."

"You can't."

"Why not?"

"Oguri's bribed the boiler room men."

"How do you know?"

"You hear things in Third Class. If the girls really are there, and you're found in that space, they'll do you in right away and toss you overboard."

"So how do we check?"

"During a storm, when things get confusing."

"What if we don't run into a storm?"

*

They ran into a storm.
Knock knock.

Nakayama moaned. He was so seasick he could not get out of his bunk. Clutching his pistol, he forced himself to sit up and lurch towards the door.

"Mr. Tachiba-aa-na?" sang a sweet female voice in English. "It's Alice Waa-aa-tson..."

Nakayama sighed in relief and unlocked the door. He hissed, "Get in here."

Sparrow glided in. She was in a magnificent lace dress of white and pink, with matching accoutrements. She wrinkled her nose. "Poor Nakayama. Have you been sick?"

"Sorry. I hate ships."

"You're with the maritime police."

"I know. And my grandfather is a retired navy admiral. If he sees me now, I shall have to commit ritual suicide."

"Can I watch?"

"No." He lay back in bed. "I hope nobody saw you coming here."

"Are you kidding, it's a ghost town out there. Everyone is in their bunk, heaving." Sparrow looked around. The tiny room had four tiny bunk beds, all of which were empty except for Nakayama's. "God, this *is* small. I've never been on a luxury liner before. So interesting how money divides people."

Nakayama said faintly, "What do you want?"

"I'm bored. Played cards with myself all morning, then decided to come see if you were still alive. I punched you a couple of times really hard. Guess I got carried away."

"You came to check on me *three days after?*"

"I didn't hear from you and got worried. Koto updated me on the mission."

"I hope he is presently executing the search plan."

"What search plan?" Sparrow clung on to the empty top bunk across from Nakayama as the ship listed precariously.

Nakayama closed his eyes. Watching Sparrow sway from side to side made him dizzy. "The one that kicks in when we run into a storm."

"You mean searching the secret compartment between the boiler rooms?"

"Exactly that."

"There are eight girls stuffed in there."

Nakayama bolted upright and hit his head. *Thunk!* "Ouch! You found them?"

"Just now. On my way to see you. Koto was busy."

"With what?" Nakayama nearly screamed. "It was *his* job to search that place!"

"No, his job is coal trimming, and the ship's listing. The coal piles are spilling all over the place and have to be shoveled back to maintain equilibrium, otherwise we'd all go down for sure. Even your police boys are too busy shoveling to do anything." She folded her gloved hands primly on her lap. "Since I was the only one with nothing to do, I went to the boiler rooms for a look. Eight girls, all Japanese. At least, they were in Japanese clothing. They could be Korean. Not Chinese because I did try to talk to them in Mandarin. They couldn't understand a word. Looked at me like I was an Angel sent from God." She lifted her dainty heeled boot and examined the fluffy hem of her skirt. "Maybe I'll keep this dress."

"Did anyone see you?"

"No. The girls are in bad shape. They'd cried their eyes out. No one's given them any food for days, and the only water they have has spilled in this storm."

Nakayama tried to get up again, coughing. "I have to execute the rest of my plan."

Sparrow leaned over and pushed him down. She sat on his bunk. "Forget it, Nakayama. It's taken care of."

"What do you mean?"

"I let them out."

"What! You'll be discovered!"

"I tell you, there is *nobody* out there. The girls and I hustled quickly upstairs to Third Class. We didn't run into a soul."

"Where are they now?"

"With my friends."

"What friends?"

"I made a lot of friends in Third Class. I've won sixteen boxing matches in a row. Including ours. My stock's pretty high you know."

"You're too visible. Oguri – "

"You're right. When the storm's over, the girls' absence will be discovered for sure. But we won't wait for the storm to be over. We need to deal with Oguri now." She nodded at the pistol, still gripped in his hand.

"No, no, I want him alive for trial," said Nakayama. The ship bucked again. He felt increasingly light-headed. "I have enough evidence now – the moment we dock in Singapore – "

"C'mon," said Sparrow, clutching at him to stop him from rolling off the bunk. "Does it really take you an American boxer from Tianjin to tell you that you won't be able to prosecute him in Singapore? I mean, for Christ's sake! It's run by the British!"

"Nothing wrong with that, I grew up in England!" said Nakayama hotly. "They are very good with enforcing the law!"

"Only for whites! They don't really care about yellows. Singapore's always been the center of the flesh trade. There's a reason the island's name begins with *Sin*. There is nothing more uninteresting to white Christians than yellow people screwing each other. Unless you're a missionary. None in the British Government last time I checked."

"I have a cooperation agreement with the British maritime police in Singapore – " began Nakayama feebly.

"Gimme a break. Didn't you say the island is seventy percent male? Singapore needs female flesh the way this ship needs to burn coal to run. You think you can keep the world's biggest pimp in jail while you arrange for his return tickets to Nagasaki? Please."

He was speechless. Then – "You'd make a good cop."

She surveyed him critically. "You know, Nakayama, you're not a bad boxer. Where'd you learn to box?"

"Harrow."

"What's that?"

"My school. In England. I had to learn to box. I was always getting bullied. I was one of two Japanese, and the other one was as tall as Koto."

She beamed. "You know in *my* temple school in Tianjin we used to make fun of all the Japanese in town because they were so irritating and tiny and perfect. The monks scolded us because they said we mustn't stereotype people. Turns out, we were spot on."

"I will throw up on you."

She opened up the little lace purse she was carrying. "Throw up in here."

He did.

She gave him her lace shawl to clean his face, then reached for a bottle rolling about the bunk. "This yours?"

"My tea."

She opened it and sniffed. "This is tea? You need whisky, my man." She drank some. "Oooh. It's awful."

"Never understood why. We're closer to India than I was in London but I can't get good Darjeeling."

"They send the best stuff over there. It's called Colonialism." She helped him drink it. "You need to try the tea in China. It's still good and I intend to make sure it stays that way."

He apologized as she capped the bottle. "No one has ever seen me this ill in my life, not even my mother. Anyway," he glared suddenly. "I grant you that I am perfect and irritating, but I'm not tiny. Why, I'm as tall as you."

"I'm considered very small by American standards. I wouldn't know. Have you been to America?"

"Only once."

"And?"

"They *were* kind of big," he admitted.

"See? I never got much milk in Tianjin growing up." She nodded again at his pistol. *"Zen'yang, faguan?* (How now, constable?)"

"Beg your pardon?"

"Got a nickname at home?"

"*Botchan*." (Young master).

"What'd they say to you in such a situation?"

"*Botchan, dō suru?*" (What do we do, Young Master?)

She repeated it with startling accuracy. His heart skipped a beat. She did not notice and continued, "If we dispose of Oguri at sea, during a storm, we can simply say he fell overboard. Accident." She grinned, Cheshire cat-like.

"Still...I can't sanction criminal behavior," he mumbled.

"Did they teach English at Harrow? What part of 'accident' do you not understand?"

He thought for a moment. "Are you up for it?"

"Me? Whoever said it was going to be me?" She raised her eyebrows in astonishment. "Koto will do it. Isn't that why you recruited him?"

"Not really. As far as I know, Koto has no record of murdering anyone."

"He has to start somewhere." Sparrow leaned closer to him. "Oguri sold his *mother* into prostitution. Probably his sister as well."

Nakayama fell silent. Then – "How do you plan on doing this?"

She took the pistol from him. "Oguri wants to meet me because he admires my boxing.

Koto and I will pay him a visit and draw him out on open deck on a pretext."

"What pretext? *I* can't think of one. In this weather?"

"I'll think of something." Sparrow smiled. "Isn't that why you recruited me?" Her smile faded. "Actually, *why* did you recruit me?"

Nakayama said nothing, just stared at her for a long time. The ship rose heavenward, then dropped twenty feet with sickening speed.

THE IMPREJARIO

Nakayama Sen was not entirely correct when he said that he had never met the great impresario, merchant, smuggler, loan-shark, brothel-owner and human trafficker Oguri Junichiro. When Nakayama was still in his mother's womb, his parents attended a lawn party thrown by the Japanese Consul in London. Many luminaries were in attendance, including Dr. Sun Yat-sen of China and, representing a union of Japanese businessmen, a younger Oguri Junichiro.

The Japanese Consul gave a long, inspirational speech about the need to "continually advance" Japan's interests around the world. Oguri, he said, was one of the few businessmen who truly understood "our modern era of global interconnectedness". He praised Oguri for doing his bit to help his country prosper in new territories. He invited Oguri to come up and make a speech introducing his union to the London community.

Nakayama's father happened to be seated next to Dr. Sun Yat-sen, who remarked that they shared the same last name. The Chinese activist had spent time in Japan. He adopted a name there, *Zhongshan*, which was read *Nakayama* in Japanese. Upon this discovery, the two men engaged in amicable discourse about books that had just come out. They commiserated on English food and weather. They avoided discussion of contemporary politics.

They broke off when Oguri finished his talk. They applauded.

"That man is a vampire," said Dr. Sun to Lieutenant Nakayama.

"He is not well thought of in some circles."

"Still, it is clever," said Dr. Sun. "Mixing some foxes in the wolf pack."

"I'm not sure I get your meaning, sir."

"One is so focused on fighting off the wolves that the foxes slide through." Dr. Sun nodded at him, still smiling. "Soldiers and merchants. You learned from the British."

"And why has China not?"

"Unlike Japan and Britain, we are not a small island nation. We will modernize, but not in the same way as you have."

Lt. Nakayama inclined his head respectfully.

Later that evening, in the carriage, his wife said, "I rather liked him!"

"Aye, you always fall for witty men."

"I usually don't like the Chinese, but if a man is witty I don't care where he's from. Honestly, if a man makes me laugh, I don't even care if he's not good-looking."

"It must follow that you were solely attracted to me for my looks."

She laughed. "Seriously, Dr. Sun's gaining quite a following."

"So I hear." Their seating arrangement at the party was not an accident. Lt. Nakayama was part of an elaborate network of Japanese military attachés (a.k.a. spies) throughout Europe. Their efforts would aid in winning two upcoming wars, one against China and another against Russia.

"Do you agree with what he said about us?" asked his wife. 'Us', of course, meant their country.

Her husband yawned. "I'm too tired to talk politics, my dear."

Her tone changed. "Don't patronize me, Masayoshi-*san*."

He was wide awake again. "Sorry."

"I was offered your job. I chose not to because *nii-san* died. If I died as well, who'd look after my parents?"

He squeezed her hand. The electricity in his wife terrified him sometimes.

She eased back into her usual self. "They say Dr. Sun's a very interesting man." She looked out the window at black figures in a wash of grey. Japan felt very far away. "*Sun Zhongshan.* What a nice name. Sounds like a bell tolling deep in the mountain." She turned around. "Do we really have to call our baby Robert or Roberta?"

But you already said yes."

"My parents wrote and said it resembles the word *Robber*. They said that sounds unlucky."

"Only people who don't speak English would even dream of making such a connection!"

They fell silent. The carriage veered around a traffic circle. She pressed her face against the window as they passed the memorial fountain. "Ah, *yappari ne.* (As I thought)," she said regretfully. "You can't see the golden Cupid in Piccadilly when it rains."

"That's not Cupid. That's his brother, Anteros."

"How do you know these things?

"Was invited to the unveiling."

"Cupid had a brother? They look exactly the same."

"Anteros was created as a playmate for Cupid so he won't be lonely," said Lt. Nakayama. "Look. Forget about an English name. Just name our baby whatever makes you happy."

"Really? What about 'Anteros'?"

"No more Western names."

"Why the sudden caving in?"

"I'll be away a lot anyway."

"True." She didn't turn from the window.

✳

Nakayama was right. Neither Sparrow nor Koto could think of a pretext of luring their prey out on open deck.

"Well, if we're going to shoot him anyway before dumping him into the ocean, it'll be easier shooting him in his room," said the boxer. "Less chances of him running way."

They were conferring in Sparrow's room in First Class, which was at the other end of the long, blue-carpeted corridor from Oguri's.

"How do we carry his body upstairs?" said Koto nervously. "It won't fit through this kind of porthole."

"We cut it up."

"With *what?*"

"Gosh, I wish I brought my sword. I had the *best* Chinese sword, real old-school, but it was so bulky to travel with." Sparrow paced around her room. She pulled off her gloves and began unlacing her heeled boots. "Hey, can you unhook me? I've got to get out of this dress."

"What are you doing?" cried Koto.

"I can't possibly go to Oguri's room dressed like I'm rich, can I? He'd find it very fishy since he saw me boxing in Manchu clothes. Anyway I can't think when I'm in this kind of clothing. Ever worn a corset? They're designed to squeeze women so that our brains stop working, otherwise we'd be so smart, we'd be running the world." She turned around and showed him a long line of tiny pearl and sateen buttons down her back. "I can hook myself up with a wire hook thing, but I can't undo it on my own. Nakayama didn't budget for a lady-in-waiting."

Gingerly he began unfastening her with the tip of his thumbs and forefingers. "Now *my* brain is going to stop working."

"Surely it's not anything you haven't seen before." She bent over as he fumbled. His fingers shook.

"You're right," she said thoughtfully. "We have nothing to cut him up. You'd need a saw. Think of the blood. But I still think we should do him in in the room. Ever killed a man?"

He shook his head miserably. "You?"

"Lived through the Boxer Rebellion in Tianjin, what do you expect? It was kill or be killed. We had to defend our temple from raiders."

"What about your parents?"

"Dead or missing, I never found out. They were in the countryside when it happened. After the dust settled, they still didn't come back or send word. I assumed the worst."

"I'd have gone to search for them!"

Sparrow grew quiet. "Yeah, you would, wouldn't you, Koto? But I'm not you."

"It's what any child would have done for their parents," he said feelingly.

"You didn't have my parents. I don't want to talk about them. I'm a million miles away. Hell if I'm going to let them haunt me on this ship!" She wriggled but still couldn't get out of the dress because he had only done half of the buttons. He told her to stay put. She said, "After the Boxer Rebellion, I decided to get out of China. I was too old to be in the temple anyway. Boxed my way down to Shanghai and stowed away on a cargo ship to Nagasaki."

"Why Nagasaki?"

"Planning to end up in Hawaii. Hurray!"

She was finally freed from the dress. Modestly, he looked out the porthole as she struggled out of her underwear and back in her comfortable Manchu jacket and pants. It was two hours to sunrise.

"What does it look like outside?" she asked, braiding her hair.

"It's murky. Perfect for body disposal. If we can somehow conceal it to carry it down this long corridor and up to deck without running into anyone."

"We're in luck." Sparrow pulled out something that looked like a thick cloth balloon from the tiny closet. "Ta-dah! Perfect body bag."

"You brought one?" he cried.

"It's the thing the stupid dress came in."

Sure enough, on the side, printed in prim gold letters:

AOISHIMA & SONS
FINE EUROPEAN TAILORING
NAGASAKI

✳

Oguri wasn't in his room. They hadn't counted on that. They were almost disappointed.

"This *is* his cabin, right?" said Sparrow.

"Cabin 8. He said," said Koto.

Quietly, Sparrow produced a hairpin and picked the lock.

"Is there anything you can't do?" said Koto.

"Math. Sssh! Keep a lookout. He might return."

Chackkk! The door swung open.

The rolling ship had made a mess of the room. Spilled drinks, clothing, even money everywhere.

Koto stepped on something. A gold watch. On the back, *April 24, 1881.*

Sparrow stared at him in shock. "Nakayama's. Seen it before."

They ran back out.

"Call his cops!" shouted Sparrow. "I'll go ahead!"

✳

The problem of enticing Oguri Junichiro upstairs to open deck was solved. The man himself was up there, in the wind and the rain, with the trim, lifeless body of Nakayama Sen casually flung across his right shoulder.

Fortunately the heaving deck made his progress slow. It also made it awfully difficult for Sparrow to get a clear shot.

Where the hell was Koto and the police?

A shout came from the darkness. It was a First Class cabin steward from the ship. She could not understand Japanese. He seemed to be urging Oguri back to the safety of below deck. Oguri turned and pulled out a pistol.

Bang!

Sparrow shot first. Oguri staggered back and dropped Nakayama. The deck slanted precariously to the right. Nakayama slid towards the ocean.

Bang! The howling wind obscured the sound. Good. Sparrow dashed right up to Oguri and emptied the rest of the rounds in him. When the gun clicked empty, she flung the murder weapon into the sea. *Waste of a perfectly good gun!* she thought.

The ship lurched forward. She clung on to the railing, then made a wild grab for Nakayama's body as it rolled towards her. She got the collar of his shirt. His feet were already over the edge. "Help!" She yelled at the steward.

He crept forward fearfully.

The ship moved again. Oguri's body rolled into the steward and tripped him up. Nakayama's shirt began to tear in her hand.

Again, the ship pitched. Oguri and the steward rolled towards Sparrow and Nakayama.

"Oh for God's sake!" she screamed. "Give me a hand here! This is the magistrate of Nagasaki!"

The steward crashed into the railing and clung on to it for dear life. He cried, "I can't let go!"

She waited for the movement of the ship, then caught its momentum and swung herself and Nakayama back to the middle of the deck.

"Sparrow!" came Koto's howl. Blurry shapes of men appeared on deck.

"We're fine!" said Sparrow. She reached for a rope swinging wildly from the life boats. She tugged at it and lashed herself and Nakayama to a nearby guardrail. "Save the steward!"

She wanted to say *I killed Oguri* but caught herself just in time. Not in front of the police.

The policemen formed a human chain and reached out to the steward.

Koto got to her first. "Is he alive?"

"Think so. He's still warm. I think he was stabbed or shot. We've got to get rid of Oguri."

"Is Oguri dead?"

"He will be if he goes overboard. Act like you're carrying him back below deck to save him. Then ditch him the moment they're not looking."

Koto nodded. She watched, quivering with adrenalin or icy cold, she wasn't sure. She didn't look away until she saw Koto shove Oguri's body over the side. He even peered over the railing, into the surf, to make sure. Despite the dangerous conditions, he stood in that manner for a long time, as if allowing the moment to sink in.

伍

BOTCHAN

"*Botchan?*"

...

"*Botchan?*"

...

A woman. It was his young English nanny. His first secret crush at age three. Oh, it was good to be back in suburban London! How he missed it, the two-story house of white stone and dove-grey shutters, the trim little front lawn with clumps of tulips, the unkempt back garden that led to a dimpled brook with banks of grassy wild garlic and dainty bluebells. That strangely mixed odor of sweet flowers, laced faintly with the threat of garlic, used to drive him crazy. How he would love to smell it again.

"Nanny," he murmured. "I ran and ran. Now I have a stitch in my side."

"It's not a stitch. You've been stabbed and sewn back up. Don't move. You've lost lot of blood."

The present came rushing back. Nakayama opened his eyes. He was in a large, First Class cabin. Nanny turned out to be – "Oh," he said, disappointed. "It's only you. Have we reached Hong Kong at least?"

"We've already did our Hong Kong stop. You were out like a light."

"What! How is it possible the storm is still on? I want to puke, but there's nothing left to throw up."

"That storm was long over," said Sparrow. "This is a new storm starting up."

"You've got to be kidding me!"

"There's a storm every day now that we're nearing Singapore. It's the tropical pressure. But don't worry. There's a very competent surgeon on board and two nurses. We're on schedule to reach Singapore tomorrow. The whole ship's excited about it."

"Don't tell my mom that I'm injured."

"Unfortunately your cops have already cabled her. She wants us to take a ship back immediately to Nagasaki but the surgeon recommends that you stay in a Singapore hospital for at least a fortnight before going back on a ship. In case complications develop. The doctor's given you some kind of emergency painkiller." Sparrow bent down and whispered. "I think it's laudanum."

"Oh God. Get me off it."

"All right. I'll tell him that. It'll be painful though."

"Koto? And the women you saved?"

"Everyone's fine except you, *botchan*. And Oguri, who's at the bottom of the sea."

"I was careless. Oguri suspected it was me when we were sparring in Third Class. He lifted the watch off me."

A gold watch appeared in Sparrow's hand. "Serves you right for giving away your watch chain!" She tucked it in his pocket.

"Oh, thank God you found it! I didn't even notice him palming it when he bumped into me. Just my luck — it is the only thing I ever carry on me that can possibly identify me. No name, just a birthdate. When I was seasick in bed and you left me to get him, he showed up."

"I'm sorry."

"Don't be. You've acquitted yourself admirably, Sparrow. You and Koto." He knew that one or both probably saved his life, but was suddenly too self-conscious to ask for the details. He was afraid he might start crying.

Sparrow studied him closely. "Why did you recruit me, *botchan*?"

"Why did you accept?"

She grinned. "I'm starving. Off to dinner, then I have to make plans with Koto about what to do about the girls when we dock."

"Send up Takuma and Kiku from my team. I'll take care of everything from here."

"Spoken like an arrogant bastard. Just shut up and lie down. I'll inform the doctor you're up. I'm having your men take turns watching you."

"Didn't you say there were two nurses on board?" he said hopefully.

She got to the door. "Yeah, but they're old and mean."

"Never mind."

✳

"Just when you thought it was all over," said Koto helplessly. He was in Third Class with a couple of Nakayama's policemen. His hair was rumpled. He was on his way to growing a full beard (his shaving mirror broke during the last storm). He scratched his chin awkwardly. "We just came back from a staff meeting of coal trimmers. The ship's Captain has noticed that a

First Class passenger, Oguri Junichiro, is missing. The ship has to report any missing passengers upon docking to the Singapore British police. All crew have been instructed to search the ship. Bottom line, if we can't produce Oguri, dead or alive, all of us we'll have to face the British police once we make landfall. The Captain says Oguri's a prominent figure in Singapore. He's afraid of trouble."

Sparrow pulled at her lower lip. "Surely people fall overboard all the time during storms? And it gets written off as a misadventure?"

Koto shrugged. "That's our backup stance. Unless we come up with a better plan."

Sparrow said suddenly, "Hey, why are you all up here? Who's trimming the coal? The ship's still listing in this storm."

"Gosh, it's been so rocky that it's my new normal. I didn't even notice," said Koto. He got up and stretched. He said in Japanese, "Let's get back to work, guys. The coal isn't going to shovel itself." He poked Sparrow in the ribs as he passed. "You and Nakayama think of something. I'm just the brawn."

"Yeah, I'm the brains and the beauty."

He sighed. "Leave something for Nakayama to do."

"Budget."

✳

Nakayama, propped up in bed, rummaged through the contents of a confiscated suitcase.

"It's no use," he said to two of his policemen. "Everything of his is way too big. Is there a tailor on board?"

"Yes, sir. This luxury liner has everything."

"Really? Get me the tailor, the men's hairdresser, and a shoemaker. And some Darjeeling tea, egg and cress sandwiches – "

"I don't think they have egg and cress. They have egg and cucumber," said the policeman, consulting the menu.

"Can't eat that. Cheese and pickle?"

"Cheese and tomato."

Nakayama pressed his hand on his mouth as if he was seasick. "Forget it. Just the tea and some whisky for my pain.

"But the doctor said…"

"No choice!" said Nakayama briskly. "The laudanum is wearing off."

A knock on the door. The policemen excused themselves. Koto and Sparrow came in.

"We heard."

"You're mad."

"I'm a man painted into a corner," said Nakayama. "That idiot Captain will not shut up until we produce Oguri."

"You look nothing like him!"

"For starters, you're way shor —"

"I am aware!" Nakayama held up his hand abruptly. He winced. "Talking makes my side hurt. I'll stack up the heels and soles of my shoes. I've sent for the shoemaker and his ilk. Although it goes against my aesthetics, I can reproduce Oguri's dated look. Once a false walrus moustache goes on, and a top hat, nobody can tell. From afar."

Sparrow stepped back and surveyed him critically. "You know, you might not be crazy after all. Once you meet Koto, you can always pick him out of a crowd, because he's just so...*Koto.* You, on the other hand, are the sort who can transform completely with a few minor adjustments."

"My mother says I have completely regular features and am thus a perfect god-like creation."

"You mean you have an eminently forgettable face."

"Don't argue with a dying man," he said, clutching his side. The wave of pain passed. "Just do as I say. I'm in charge."

"Until you're seasick," said Sparrow.

Nakayama said to Koto, "Don't you *ever* tire of her?"

陆

ſIN CITY

There was always a tremendous amount of confusion whenever a passenger ship docked in Singapore. Everyone would try to get off at once, in no particular order. A stormy week at at sea seemed to have robbed all passengers of the ability to form sentences, let alone queues. Many were ill from the rocky passage and had to be carried off on stretchers or, when not available, deck chairs. Adding to the chaos was the trooping on board of scores of half-naked coolies wearing long Qing braids coiled around their heads. Their sole purpose was to unload everything in Cargo.

Cargo logistics were completely unrelated to passengers' proceedings. The coolies were paid solely based on the speed at which they could complete their work. In an era where British medical authorities cautioned against having a British soldier bear a load exceeding 30% of his body weight, the Chinese coolie carried towering sacks of grain that was 100% of his own weight. This feat was accomplished with nothing more than a small towel on his back to prevent his bare skin from being rubbed raw by burlap. Sullen, efficient, he would crash into anyone in his way without apology, knocking hats off or worse.

Customs and immigration in Singapore consisted of a few wooden counters and Sikh guards in a squat brick building. Some people simply waltzed through the checkpoint, others were stopped and mercilessly stripped and searched. There appeared to be no rhyme or reason to the proceedings. The signs were in English, a language nobody appeared to actually speak or read. So *Do Not Cross* would be exactly at the point in the bustling street where everybody crossed, and *Do Not Spit* would be exactly where everybody found it convenient to spit. Of course, *No Solicitation* was a joke. Touts and pickpockets converged upon the foreign arrivals, especially on well-dressed women.

"Fascinating," said Nakayama Sen in a low voice as he made his way down the gangplank. He was resplendent in new togs as the *zegen* Oguri Junichiro. His prior identity, Japanese boxer "Tachibana", who (if anybody remembered) was en route to an exhibition match at a Singapore hotel, had evaporated into thin air. The Captain and crew did not care. Nobody really kept count of Third Class as long as fares were paid.

Sparrow (dressed as "Alice Watson") was already waiting for him impatiently at the bottom of the gangplank, perspiring under her parasol, which doubled as a tout-basher. "What took you so long?"

"These shoes are so weird," said Nakayama.

"You're gonna trip and fall."

"Stop drawing attention to me, would you?" he said, annoyed.

"We're supposed to go round to the other side and meet everyone else there. They get off at the other gangplank."

"I see them," said Nakayama cheerfully, straining to catch a glimpse over the crowd. "They've got the eight girls, too. Good job. We all made off in one piece. Gosh, high heels are amazing. I can see over the tops of more heads. I shall wear them always." He offered her an arm. "Shall we?"

She accepted it warily. Nakayama expressed delight at their new relative height. "So refreshing," he said. "I've always wanted to bend down to kiss a girl. Unfortunately most girls are exactly my height, so I've never wanted to kiss them. Ever had that problem?"

"I don't know whether to laugh or cry," said Sparrow, deadpan.

Koto waved in the distance. They struggled past haranguing touts and peddlers to get to him.

"*Danna! Danna! Chotto...Oguri-san!*" came a woman's cry.

Nakayama froze.

"Surely," he said between clenched teeth. "He hadn't arranged *to be met at the docks by somebody?*"

"Just keep walking," said Sparrow, smiling and nodding at Koto in the distance. "She'll come round and see your face, realize she's mistaken and move on."

A young woman in kimono, followed by a maid with a paper umbrella, came clattering up breathlessly to Nakayama. She wore a lot of makeup and hair accessories. Was she a geisha? In *Singapore?* Nakayama stopped short.

"Oguri-san!" she hugged him. Her hair ornaments tinkled merrily. "Thank goodness you're safe! We have a rickshaw waiting. Come on, everyone's been waiting for this, we were so afraid you'd be delayed at sea!" She noticed Sparrow for the first time. She flapped her hands, shooing her away as if she was a stray puppy. "Oh, Oguri-san, you've been naughty again with foreign women, haven't you! Wait till you see what new ladies we've got on Hylam Street. Come on now! My boy will pick up your luggage, we can go ahead."

Nakayama shook his head imperceptibly at Sparrow and allowed himself to be led away to the street where a line of rickshaws waited.

Koto came up and took off his cap, astonished. "What the hell?" He fanned himself.

Sparrow was appalled. "She thought he was Oguri. Doesn't make sense. She's either stupid or cunning."

"What do we do?"

"She mentioned a street called Hylam."

"It's one of the red-light districts. I'll tail them."

"But – "

"This is my town. You take care of the girls. Send his men after us, but discreetly."

"Don't lose sight of him. He really should be in hospital."

"Leave it to me."

✳

Koto wove through the crowds at the landing docks. His eyes never left Nakayama and the woman. Now that he was back home, he felt a new sense of purpose.

"Hylam Street," he said, leaping into a rickshaw. He handed the rickshaw man a generous amount of money. "Quickly!"

With a sickening lurch he was en route.

Botchan has never been to Singapore before, thought Koto worriedly.

"You from Japan, friend?" asked the rickshaw man in broken English.

"Nah, I'm a Chinese like you," replied Koto in the local dialect. He often invoked whichever half he thought would get him better service.

"Heh heh! The moment you're off the ship, you head for Hylam Street!" the rickshaw man cackled. "For the foreign sailors, I have to force them to go, but for you, you're willingly jumping into the fire!"

"Actually, that's not what I – " began Koto hastily.

"It's okay, it's okay! Your first time, big bro?"

"Um, yes. I'm a bit nervous." Koto was in information-gathering mode. He had learned, in the past year, that he could make people tell him stuff if he played up his disingenuous appearance. "Why do you have to force foreign sailors to go to Hylam Street? I heard they go to such places all the time."

"Yeah, but you haven't heard the latest. The British Navy's put a stop to their sailors coming to Singapore for sex. The men were told Hong Kong's cleaner. So they go blow their wad in Hong Kong. By the time they sail down here they don't want to go to *our* red light district. These days the brothel owners have to pay us to magic them there. We pretend we're taking the sailors downtown shopping, then we swing right into the red-light district and abandon them! The brothel owners take it over from there."

"I see."

"So! What are you in the mood for tonight? Need a quick summary of what's available? Hylam's mostly Japanese – good choice, they're cleaner. You can have Thai, Indian, Malay too. Singapore's a good place for sampling: lots of options, all in one spot. If you can afford it, definitely try a European before you leave town. They're the only ones who tend to get regular check-ups. They can show you a certificate of health. Signed, officially, by the Colonial Surgeon. The girls keep that certificate like it's gold! They can charge more if they produce it. If you have enough money you can ask for virgins. But there's a lot of fraud these days. You *have* to make sure you get blood, otherwise you can ask for your money back. Since you gave me such a good tip, I have to warn you – leave the Chinese girls for cheapskates like me. They're an awful lot. Most of them are sick as hell. The government doesn't check them at all, even though there are more Chinese prostitutes than all other races combined!"

"That's crazy," said Koto despairingly. It was the first time he heard this tidbit. "No wonder the diseases spread."

"The Brits say there are too many Chinese girls. Their hospitals would be overwhelmed. So they advise their soldiers to stick to foreign prostitutes and leave the Chinese girls for the Chinese. That's how they're containing the spread of disease in this town. Makes sense, doesn't it? In a sick way. So for men like me, it's like playing Russian roulette!"

"Damn right."

"You're new, you don't know how it works here. See, to the British government, we Chinese, we're like rats. We fuck too much, breed too much, spread all these diseases. But they keep letting more of us in, 'cos the system needs us. We keep the city running. The goods on those ships ain't gonna unload themselves. And this pair of legs, it helps them get from point A to point B for cheap!" The rickshaw man ran faster through the traffic, as if to demonstrate his prowess. "Anyway, it's easy for them to look down on us. They can afford so many refined things. For men like us, sex is the only pleasure left in life. Cheaper than opium. I'd marry but there's not enough women. It's a damned sausage party over here!"

Koto had been silent all this time, his eyes glued to the back of Nakayama's rickshaw. He was afraid of losing sight of it.

Botchan, this is all my fault, thought Koto helplessly. I was so idealistic. I thought if I could get to Japan, I would stop the human trafficking at its source. The British had given up trying to stop it here, so I thought...I thought...I heard you give your speech in public the day you assumed office. There was something about your manner. I thought you might listen to me. So I told you about Oguri, about the girls smuggled in the holds of ships. I sent you all the information that I had uncovered. I hoped that someday, someone in the authorities would investigate. I didn't think you would get involved so quickly and so personally. *Botchan*, what have I done!

They reached the row of towering, three-story shophouses with balconies and lanterns.

"Stop here, stop here," said Koto breathlessly. He handed the rickshaw man more money. "Thanks."

"Eh, you already paid me at the beginning." He wiped his face with his towel.

But Koto had disappeared quickly into the crowd.

✳

"Yuki, 14."
"Sayuri, 19."
"Yayoi, 18."
"Natsuko, 17."
"Yukino, 18."
"Reiko,18."
"Hina, 12."
"Hanae, 13."

Sparrow watched as Nakayama's police deputy, Takuma, wrote down the girls' particulars. Some had family names, others were too poor to have any such designation. The younger ones did not even know how to write their own names. They were all from Amakusa and Shimabara, the twin tributaries of a mighty human river that dumped its contents into Singapore.

Takuma asked, "Do you know who would be meeting you at the docks?"

"There was a man in Western dress with a big moustache."

"Yes, yes, we know about him. But anybody else? Got any names?"

They conferred with each other and shook their heads. They were eating noodle soup at the open air market. The ones who had finished were polishing off ice lollies that

Sparrow had bought them. They seemed to have recovered from their ordeal and were eager to go home.

Takuma's assistant, Kiku, returned. He had a stack of tickets. "The *Ko Maru* sails for Nagasaki day after tomorrow. It's the soonest available." He distributed the tickets. "Sparrow-*san*, eight of my men will accompany them each back to their hometowns. They will pretend to be couples on board the ship so that no questions are asked." He blushed a little, as if on the verge of saying something else, then decided against it.

Sparrow licked her ice cream cone. "What's the point of returning them to their hometowns if they'll just be shanghaied again by another crook?"

"Do you have a better plan? They can't stay here. They don't speak the language. They'll die here, or worse."

One of the girls tugged at his sleeve and said something. He nodded. "They said they'll spread word about their kidnapping and warn the other girls once they get back to their village. They're willing to take the risk. They don't want anybody to go through what they've been through."

Another girl spoke up.

"They asked if there were other girls from their village who may have been kidnapped here."

"Yeah, I'm sure," said Sparrow.

An excited discussion ensued, with a lot of nodding, *ne's,* and sounds of vigorous assent between the two prim, plainclothes policemen and the village girls in ragged kimono, with their hair standing up in fuzzy pigtails in the humidity. It made for a rather comic sight.

Takuma composed himself and said in careful English, "Of the eight girls, two have elected to stay in Singapore. Sayuri, age 19, and Hina, age 12. The oldest and the youngest."

"Why?"

"Sayuri's family is destitute. If she goes back she'll either starve or be sold to someone as a slave. Hina is an orphan living with a grandmother who beats her and doesn't give her enough to eat. There's a drought in her village. If she goes back she'll starve anyway. They're willing to take their chances here. They ask if you, Koto, and Nakayama *taicho* would be in the new country with them."

"No. Koto wants to go to Amakusa. I've never been to Singapore and there is no reason for me to stay. As for Nakayama, he's the magistrate of Nagasaki, for Christ's sake." Sparrow said bluntly. "They're on their own if they don't take the fare back."

The oldest girl made a long speech and bowed.

"She says she wants to stay and help rescue other girls from Shimabara. It would give her a purpose. She's a Catholic convert and had always wanted to work as a missionary or a nurse. She and Hina have decided to be adopted sisters. She'll take care of Hina. She adds that the passage was so rough that it felt like being in Purgatory. She will not survive another ship journey. Thus, please give her permission to stay."

Sparrow looked at the group. "*Me?* It's not up to me. I'm not in charge here."

"Excuse me, but Nakayama *taicho* says if anything happened to him, we will temporarily take orders from you until we return to Nagasaki. *Chotto*, I forgot," said Takuma. He fumbled in his pocket and pulled out a little red velvet bag with gold writing printed on it. "Here," he held it up to her nose with both hands and bowed. "His seal. He wanted you to have it. It gives you authority."

"What! Was he planning to die?"

"No. It didn't go with his Oguri costume."

Sparrow accepted the bag warily. "Are you guys *really* the Japanese Maritime Police?"

"Yes. We're the best team. Special Executions."

"Well, Special Ex," said Sparrow, surveying the neighborhood. "It's getting too hot for words. Any ideas of how we can get a cheap hotel to fit all of us for the night? I'm desperate for a bath."

THE BLUE POPPY
LAUNDRY SHOP

Koto finally found a weird boarding house near the Singapore River that was willing to take a big group for a couple of nights. It fit their dwindling budget. It was a large, two-story building. The ground floor resembled a large, airy gymnasium filled with Indian boys competing in board games called *carrom*. There were dozens of boards on the floor, with a gaggle of shouting brown bodies around each. Slippers piled high at the entrance. The upstairs, accessible through a flight of narrow, dingy stairs, was divided into little dormitory rooms, each with a cotton curtain for a door. Everybody shared a single kitchen and washing area. The toilets were downstairs, in a makeshift outhouse. One peed and pooped into tin potties, which were removed and changed for new tin potties every morning by two men in a bullock cart called the "night soil carriers". This was a service provided by the municipal authorities for a fee.

Sparrow and the eight girls adapted quickly. It was the Nagasaki policemen who were upset by the conditions, having been used to superior infrastructure back home. They ran around excitedly, pointing out all the things that were different. They bought street food and shared it around. Finally they wore themselves out in the heat and flopped down, exhausted, in their rooms, only to be stung by mosquitoes.

Koto and some of the policemen had gone after Nakayama. They had not returned by nightfall. Sparrow was about to strike out in search of them when they suddenly returned in a single hot, irritable bundle at the back of a bullock cart.

"What happened?" she cried.

"He's alive," said Koto tiredly. They had been caught in a tropical downpour. He peeled off his wet shirt and went to the wash area. He turned on the tap. "Two of our cops are keeping the house he's in under surveillance." He splashed water liberally on himself.

"I need to get him to a hospital."

"We managed to speak to him, he said he's fine, he doesn't feel any pain. He will change the dressing himself. He told us he's in the thick of investigations and to just hold on for now. He'll send for us when the time is right."

"In the thick of investigations?" Sparrow raged. "In a brothel? A likely story."

"Oh, he's not in a brothel. He's in a laundry shop. It's called The Blue Poppy Laundry Shop. That geisha lady apparently runs it. We asked around. Her business launders the sheets and *yukata* for the Japanese brothels in the area." Koto shrugged. "Of course, if she knows Oguri that well, there might a whole lot of stuff getting laundered besides the sheets."

"I'd say! So what are we all supposed to do? Wait till he sends for us? Next week? Next month?" Sparrow paced around angrily. "The team is shipping out Friday on the *Ko Maru*. Doesn't he want to go home with them?"

"We'll have a better idea tomorrow morning. My brain's too melted in this heat to strategize."

"I've half a mind to get on a ship to Hawaii if I can find one. I'd rot and die here."

"I'd stay if I were you. White people get ahead in this town. You'd be at the top of the heap. Plus, we saved you this. Somebody was giving them out." Koto handed her a flyer.

WORLD BOXING
Exhibition Match at The Raffles Hotel
Saturday Night 6 O'Clock Sharp
Fine Dining & Cigars During Match
Tickets Please Inquire At The Office

"Where's this place?" asked Sparrow.

"Nearby. Huge, super fancy. They've just added a new building: talk of the town."

"How do I get in?"

"Since you're white and have that nice dress, I could get you a ticket if you have the cash."

"Ticket? What good is a ticket? I don't want to *watch*. Can I take part?"

"Take part in what?"

Sparrow raised her fists in a perfect stance. "Find out."

"Aw, man!" groaned Koto, climbing the stairs tiredly. The night was full of cicadas. In the hall, the unmistakable sound of *carrom's* wooden counters slamming against varnished board. The laughter, shouts and cracking noises would continue till dawn. That was the reason why nobody rented the dorm rooms upstairs. "Nakayama was right. One *does* tire of you."

"If I win you get half."

"Sixty/forty."

"Fifty-one/forty-nine. After all, you didn't do anything except pick up a flyer."

"Sixty/forty or nothing."

✳

Friday came and went. Koto took time off to visit his adopted family, who ran a shop somewhere west of downtown. He came back just in time for a tearful parting at the docks. Six of the girls boarded the *Ko Maru* with six police escorts.

The four cops that were left took turns keeping The Blue Poppy Laundry Shop under round-the-clock surveillance.

Koto, incredibly, managed to get Sparrow a placement in the exhibition match by introducing his "White Female Celebrity Fighter" to the manager of the hotel, who thought the concept very classy. The subject of a gender-appropriate boxing costume was discussed. The hotel decided to market her as *Jin Que* (Golden Sparrow), a white orphan raised by Chinese monks from Shaolin, which was nowhere near Tianjin. She would fight an Indian woman boxer (apparently there was at least one in Singapore). The ring would be set up right in the middle of the Grand Ballroom. The occasion would be strictly black tie.

"There has never been anything like it!" cried the hotel manager enthusiastically. "If it sells, I'm going to organize a whole series for you."

✳

In the middle of the night, Koto woke to the sound of a woman crying quietly. The partition between the rooms was paper thin, and the doors only cloth curtain.

Was it Sparrow? No, it came from the room on the other side. He got up to go to the bathroom. He shuffled past the curtain. He said quietly, "Sayuri-*san?*"

"*Hai,*" she replied softly.

"*Daijo'ka?*" (Everything ok?)

"*Hai.*" (Yes)

"You're going home. You have your ticket. It's real and paid for. No one's going to take it away from you."

A pause, then, once again, a robotic, quiet "*Hai.*"

He sighed. He never had any sisters, so he didn't know the best way to deal with these girls. At least the younger ones could play with him, but the ones Sayuri's age were inscrutable, even terrifying. He was about to shuffle away.

"Koto-*san*."

"*Nani?*"

Sayuri lifted the curtain. "Are you going to the toilet?"

"Yes."

"I've been dying to go. Can I go with you? I'm too scared."

"Of course," he was astonished. "You could have woken Hina up. Isn't she in your room?"

"She wants to go too. We're both too scared. The black men, there are so many downstairs. They are still playing their games."

"Ah! They're Indian boys, they're not even men, don't worry about them." Koto had grown up here. "Have you never seen Indians before?"

Hina popped out from under the curtain. She was wide awake. "No! Are they ghouls? Is this what the Devil looks like?"

Koto had forgotten that they were from rural islands. "They're human, just like you and me. They're all right. If you spoke English like me, you could talk to them."

They went down together, carefully feeling their way in the half-light. The stairs creaked.

Downstairs, the *carrom* players smacked and slammed away. Some looked up briefly and nodded at Koto, who raised a hand. When they got to the outhouse, the tin door banged open and a skinny Indian boy, wearing only pajama pants, darted out. Sayuri and Hina both screamed. He looked at them and screamed back histrionically, then ran off, giggling.

"All right, girls, who's going first?" said Koto, yawning.

"You first," said Sayuri demurely.

"No, no, I'll stay guard outside. Then when you both done, I'll walk you upstairs, *then* I'll come back down and pee."

Little Hina looked relieved. "*Yokatta!* (Thank goodness)" She sighed. "I was so worried about waiting outside alone with Sayuri while you were in there peeing, *nii-chan!*"

"Thank you," said Sayuri, going in and quickly closing the door behind her. "God will bless a good person like you, Koto-*san*."

"Yeah, yeah," said Koto, yawning. "Just don't make me do it five times a night."

✳

Saturday night.

Takuma showed up at the Raffles Hotel and found Koto at the back of the ballroom. "Nakayama *taicho* wants to see you."

"Dammit!" cried Koto. "It's Sparrow's turn next! His timing is incredible. *You* go, I'm stuck here."

"He requested you specifically. He said Sparrow would be too conspicuous on Hylam Street, so you alone must go.""

Koto fumed. He went to speak to Sparrow, but she was already in the boxing ring. She wore a tight-fitted 'Boxing Panda' costume, with matching leather mask, which she got to keep if she won. He waved at her.

"Na-ka-ya-ma," he mouthed.

She cupped one of her Panda ears with a bright red boxing glove. She didn't understand.

Desperate, he mimed a saintly look, hands clasped in prayer, then pretended to pat the head of someone slightly shorter than him. *Botchan.*

She understood right away.

He made with his index and middle fingers the universal symbol for walking. She nodded and waved for him to go. She threw a few practice punches in the air and hopped around. If she was worried, Koto couldn't tell. You never can tell with Pandas.

"Ladies and Gentlemen – we round up the night with a special guest star all the way from Shaolin, China..."

✳

Poom!
Piu! Piu!

Poom!

Gunshots. Screams. Whistles of the police. Slippers, slapping frantically on pavement. Someone raised a large knife in the air.

Hylam Street on Saturday night was crammed with merrymaking. The crowd parted for the police.

Koto felt a hand on his shoulder. "This way."

"*Botchan*! I thought you were in that mob!"

"Nah, that's just normal murder. Happens every night."

Nakayama led Koto to The Blue Poppy Laundry Shop. On the tiled floor, mounds and mounds of crumpled sheets and clothing. Playing among the mounds were several dirty little girls and boys.

"She never actually does the laundry," Nakayama said drily, indicating with a sweep of his hand. "It's a front for Oguri."

"*Money* laundering?"

"You got it."

"Whose babies are these?" Koto stepped over a sleeping child.

"Prostitutes dump their kids here for Plum to look after. She doesn't. They can't hurt themselves rolling about the laundry. Come, my office is upstairs."

"Your *office*?" Then again, Koto was no longer shocked by anything Nakayama did. But the magistrate had only been gone three days. "Sparrow says you should be in hospital."

"I'm fine. Plum has tons of opium."

"Plum's the woman who carted you off at the docks?"

"Yep. She runs this shop."

"I thought you refused to take opium."

"It's just to tide me over until I can get myself a real doctor. I'm changing the dressing daily."

The 'office' was actually a beautiful little room entirely tiled and decorated in a Straits Chinese style. Hanging plants and Chinese brush paintings everywhere. Koto smelled incense. There was an tiny shrine in a corner dedicated to a green and red-painted Chinese god. A little tea set and clay stove sat in the corner. A day bed dominated the room. On it, a hard pillow of red lacquer. Koto was invited to sit on a blue and white ceramic bench.

"This is Oguri's office," said Nakayama. He wore a brand new Chinese silk jacket with hand-made frog buttons. On his feet, comfortable silk slippers. He looked like he'd moved in permanently.

"So they still think you're Oguri? Don't they know what he looks like?"

Nakayama made a new pot of tea. "I've discovered that Oguri Junichiro isn't a man."

Koto blurted, "He's a *woman* in disguise?" He thought of Sparrow.

"No. Oguri doesn't exist. He's a concept. The name is held by a different individual depending on the time. That's why he never has his photograph taken. That's why he was never caught. He is a phantom."

"No. It can't be. He's a real guy, he's famous!"

"There probably was a real man called Oguri Junichiro once, perhaps the very first. But people tend to lead short, violent lives in this industry. He probably was assassinated. His successors took turns bearing this famous name and running a business empire, which, as we know, now spans the Pacific." He poured tea in a little clay cup for Koto. "We've run into something big. Much bigger than I ever thought. I've discovered in the last three days that there are Amakusa and Shimabara girls as far as Perth and San Francisco. They got there all through Singapore. Through Oguri's network, which touches some of the wealthiest families in Japan. This, Koto, runs directly into the highest levels of government. I'm telling you because I need you to be very careful with this information. Oguri's business is part of our official colonial expansion program. Exporting manpower is easier than having to feed the mouths at home. The girls are told by Oguri that it is their filial duty to go abroad, open their legs, send money home, and do their part for their parents and for the Emperor."

Here he stopped. The money the girls sent home contributed to the Japanese effort against Russia in the spectacularly-successful war just the year before. His father was currently in New York in an official capacity, celebrating the victory with American Jewish elites who had contributed funds to Japan to fight Russia. The sex acts of poor Chinese dock workers in Singapore, the vengeful sorrow of victims of Russian pogroms, converted to bullets and cannons against the Russians. Money connected the world in ways that Koto could not imagine. So Nakayama did not elaborate further.

"But the girls we rescued from the *Tobi Maru* were kidnapped!" raged Koto. "They didn't sign up for this colonial expansion program!"

"Well, at first they were recruited to 'work at inns' which turned out to be brothels. This went on for decades. Before you and I were born. But when demand in Singapore grew, they started grabbing them right off the beaches."

"Hina is only twelve years old," said Koto bitterly.

"Well, Plum claims they don't start them off till they're 15."

"As if that makes it any better!"

"They get groomed first. Clients then offer to pay for them at age 15, 16, 17. Different prices, of course." Nakayama pulled a sheet off his office desk. "Here is the latest pricing chart. You pay for the extent to which you violate their virginity. There is the *Trying the Flower* stage, the *Opening the Flower* stage, and the *Picking the Flower* stage."

Koto turned red. "I have no idea what they're talking about."

"You've never...?"

"No."

"Me neither," said Nakayama, tossing the sheet back on his desk. Then he said hastily, "TELL SPARROW I'M A VIRGIN AND YOU DIE."

"Why would I tell Sparrow this kind of thing!" said Koto indignantly.

"This price sheet is for trying out the boys," said Nakayama, handing him another paper. "Less demand, hence cheaper."

"God!"

"Good thing your mother gave you away."

Koto refused to touch the paper offered to him.

Nakayama indicated the shelves above his desk. "These are all their ledgers and records of their criminal activities in Singapore. There are lists of the ships that bear the girls here, and the ships that export them elsewhere. In the safe I found stacks of medical certificates. The girls can't read. Plum tells them that those certificates are their official prostitution 'licenses' without which they would be caught and put in jail. Since they were smuggled here, the girls have no other forms of identification. Plum holds on to the certificates to prevent them from running away."

"That woman is so evil!"

"Well, only because they did it to her. She knows exactly how to play to those girls' fears." Nakayama looked at the stacks of papers in wonder. "How I wish I could have these papers all moved someplace safe to build a case. But I can't move without incurring suspicion."

"So what are you going to do now? Why do they think you are Oguri?"

"Plum knew I wasn't Oguri when she picked me up at the docks. We had killed that man, if you remember."

"As if I could forget!"

"She knew something was afoot, but she didn't see the real Oguri come off the ship, so she grabbed me and brought me back here for an explanation. She held a meeting of all the Japanese stakeholders last night. Hpmh! What a great lot *that* was. I told them my real identity. They've heard my name: Nagasaki's one of their key ports. I said I killed the prior Oguri because I wanted to usurp his place. I said I was ruthless and corrupt, I wished to join their network and profit from their gains. In return, I will never prosecute, in fact I would aid, their activities in Nagasaki port."

"They *believed* you?"

"Father always said, when telling a lie, make it outrageous."

"What kind of work does your old man do again?"

"He's a diplomat. He goes around the world." Nakayama poured him another cup of tea.

Koto grunted. "You mean he's a spy."

"Nonsense. Right now he's arranging a Japanese calligraphy exhibit in New York."

"But how long are you going to be Oguri?"

"Until the next one bumps me off."

"Gosh. Why are you doing this?"

"As long as I am Oguri, I can gather evidence against those in government who've got their fingers in this nasty pie. I want to know who in Tokyo's involved."

"But even if you have the evidence, who'd listen to you?"

"It'll take time. I have friends I can bring to my side."

"You'll get yourself killed, you idiot!"

"I could do nothing," said Nakayama evenly. "I could go back to fining sailors for brawls at the harbor back home. I didn't go to Harrow and Cambridge so that I could come home and be a petty bureaucrat."

"What's a Cambridge?"

"Never mind. Look, we can't save the girls here. But we can stop them from being kidnapped at their source. Wasn't that your idea? Don't you want to do something about it in Amakusa?"

Koto nodded.

"Where's Sparrow?" asked Nakayama suddenly.

"Boxing. At the Raffles Hotel."

"Who's winning?"

"No idea, she went up just when you sent for me."

"Sorry." He looked at his gold pocket watch. "Plum may be back soon. Convey the news to Sparrow and the rest. There is a ship bound for Nagasaki on Tuesday, the *Kaze Maru*. Get us all tickets. Do you have enough money left?"

"Probably not enough to get everyone First Class. Takuma said you spent all your law enforcement budget on your Oguri costume and your special high heel shoes. Come to think of it, you even had a dress tailored for Sparrow! I'*m* the only one on the mission who didn't get fine clothes."

"That's because you are always magnificent as you are, Koto-*kun*."

"Yeah right. Sayuri and Hina are staying in Singapore. The rest went back yesterday with police escorts. That leaves you, me, Sparrow, four policemen. I can get us all Third Class, tops."

Nakayama unlocked the safe and pulled out a stack of cash. "No more coal trimming. We sail in style."

Koto turned pale. "I'd rather trim coal than use blood money."

Nakayama stared. Then he put the cash back in the safe. "Very well. We will all go Third. Make the arrangements. It's all in your hands now."

As Koto turned to go, Nakayama said, "Wait." He handed Koto an envelope. "This is the information you have been searching for."

Inside, birth certificates.

Nakayama said gently, "Thank you for keeping me sane. I knew there was a reason I recruited you."

"Yeah, yeah," said Koto, blushing again. "Don't get yourself killed, *botchan*."

"See you on the *Kaze Maru*."

ſOME ARE EATEN

"See you on the *Kaze Maru*."

✳

"'Course he would be late," said Sparrow.

"If he doesn't show up, I'm getting off," said Koto.

"So will we," said Takuma and Kiku.

"I won't," said Sparrow resolutely. "I'm staying put. And upgrading to First Class with my prize money." She had, after all, made off like a bandit at the Raffles. "I simply don't understand why we have to travel Third. Once you get used to First, you can't go back to Third."

"But if we're not on board, why don't you stay as well?" said Koto. "Didn't you get two offers of marriage at that hotel? One of those guys seemed pretty legit, too."

"Who, the Turk?"

"No – the British writer."

"What, just because someone bought me a drink I have to marry him? How'd you know he doesn't have a wife back in England?"

Koto shrugged. "I'd stay in Singapore if I were you. Why'd you go back to Japan?"

"To wait for you guys to show up, of course."

"I thought you wanted to go to Hawaii?"

"That's *later*," Sparrow was evasive. "Maybe next spring."

"Where on earth is Nakayama *taicho*?" bleated Kiku worriedly. "Look! They're rolling back the gangplanks in Third."

"Relax. They always leave the ones in First for longer," said Sparrow. "Hey look! That's Sayuri and Hina, waving! Near the ice-cream man!"

They leaned over and screamed their names. "SAAAAA-YUUUU-RIIII! HINA-CHAAAAN! KIYO-TSUKETE NEEEEEE!" (TAKE CARE OF YOURSELF!)

The two girls waved wildly with both arms until they were exhausted. Takuma asked Sparrow where she had relocated them.

"Saint Anthony's Convent," Sparrow nodded in satisfaction. "Run by a bunch of nice Portuguese nuns. Canossians."

"*Convent?*" Koto was aghast. He had been nursing a chaste admiration for Sayuri. They had exchanged promises to write letters, etc. He had been looking forward to stretching this tender and secret epistolary relationship over multiple years – "Did...did Sayuri-*san* say she is going to be a nun?"

"They're *not* going to be nuns, silly!" Sparrow was impatient. "School, they're going to school! The nuns founded a school for orphan girls of all ages."

"Phew. Do they teach kungfu?" asked Koto.

"No, but Sayuri and Hina are gonna learn English. And Sayuri's gonna be our Woman in Singapore for the next mission," said Sparrow.

"The *next mission?*" chorused Koto, Takuma, and Kiku incredulously.

"Yep. I'm the temporary magistrate of Nagasaki, I get to decide," she said, brandishing Nakayama's seal in its little velvet bag. "Sayuri's gonna be a great spy. Hina, I'm keeping her on the shelf for later."

"You might have to be the permanent magistrate, if Nakayama *taicho* doesn't show up," said Takuma fearfully. Two sailors walked over to untie the gangplank for First Class passengers.

"Look!" shouted Kiku.

"Nakayama *taicho!*"

Sparrow ran to stop the sailors undoing the gangplank. Koto clattered down it.

Nakayama rode a gaunt white bullock. It had a pair of long horns that curved strangely upward so that they almost met in a vertical knot on the top of its head. He held on to them for balance. The animal was led by an elderly man, equally skinny, who held a rope attached to the ring in the bullock's nose. No two beings could possibly move slower on God's earth.

"Hurry, Nakayama *taicho!*" screamed his men.

"Hi there," Nakayama waved lazily. "I couldn't find a rickshaw at rush hour."

"RUN FOR IT!" shouted Sparrow from the deck.

Koto, who was closer to him, realized that Nakayama was in pain. "Your wound?" he asked.

Nakayama nodded.

"I'll carry you." Koto offered his back. "Quick!"

"So embarrassing in public." But he got on gingerly.

Koto hurried with his load up the gangplank. Some passengers cheered him on merrily.

✳

"Seven days in the same cabin as you two," said Nakayama. "Kill me now."

Sparrow changed his bandages. Having suffered many injuries herself from boxing, she was a bandaging expert. She retorted, "You told us to book you in Third!"

"When I travel Third, I order an entire cabin of four bunks for *myself*."

"Well, you weren't clear in your instructions," said Koto defensively. He was in the top bunk. The cabin was so small that he could reach out and touch Nakayama in the opposite bunk below. The only nice thing about the cabin was the tiny red-and-white gingham curtains on the single porthole. "Anyway, this way we have spending money for beer and chips."

"I don't understand how the stitches opened up like that," said Sparrow.

"I moved too rigorously."

"You better not move like that again, now that the doctor's sewn you back up."

"No chance of that in this cabin." Nakayama winked at Koto.

Koto tried hard not to laugh.

Sparrow looked at Nakayama, then at Koto, then back at Nakayama. "Private joke?"

"Sort of."

Koto said, giggling, "On your last night?"

"Yeah, after you left, Plum had a surprise big party that went on till Sunday morning."

Koto kept chortling.

"Would you stop," complained Nakayama. "For someone born in that area, you are a total prude!"

"I *was* born there. But I was properly raised elsewhere by my very Catholic adopted parents."

"Explains a lot! And mind you, I didn't solicit. But if offered, I would take. After all, I am Oguri Junichiro. I have no choice but to play the part."

"Tee hee hee!"

"Oh my God," said Sparrow in sudden horror.

"Don't look so shocked," said Nakayama ingratiatingly. "If you hang out with men all the time, you have to get used to men-talk."

"No, I just realized I should be more careful! Hey, Koto, can you change his dressing from now on?" She reached for a bar of soap in the tiny sink. "Syphilis can be transmitted through blood."

"Syphilis?" cried Nakayama.

"Yeah, I read in the paper yesterday when I was at the Raffles Hotel. It's the number one health crisis in Singapore right now. The British medical authorities report that more than half of the upper class Chinese families are infected with syphilis. The husbands bring it home from Hylam Street to their wives, who pass it on congenitally to the children. And that's the upper class we're talking about, let alone everybody else down the totem pole."

"B-but there was a medical certificate," mumbled Nakayama. "It looked genuine."

"No doubt. But the article said many girls share one certificate. They only have names on them, no photos – how do you know whose it really is?" Sparrow scrubbed her hands briskly with a towel. "Gosh. I tend to get cuts on my hands from boxing. I would get infected by you if I touch your bandages. Think of how awful that'll be! I'd be unmarriageable! And I'd never clear my name!"

"But I haven't felt any tingling sensation," said Nakayama feebly.

"Oh, that's other venereal diseases. Syphilis is different. The article said that it doesn't manifest immediately: it's a silent killer. It lurks in you for a full month before you notice the large lesions appearing at the – you know –

point of contact. They could be this size," she made a circle with her finger. "Some could be *this* size. You wouldn't know for a month. Meanwhile you would have infected a lot more people. That's why it's now an epidemic. Long term, it even causes madness and suicide."

"Did you save the article?" asked Koto anxiously.

"No, why would I do that? Nobody I knew would be at risk for such a disease," said Sparrow. "Well, that's what I *thought*. I should have figured that the *magistrate* of Nagasaki, our local *judge*, would visit prostitutes in Singapore and contract *venereal disease*. As the monks used to tell me, one cannot expect cops to both *fight* crime and not be affected by *sin*."

"Why are you talking in that funny way," said Nakayama in a small voice.

She rose abruptly, frowning. "I'm going to the galley to ask for hot water. I really would feel more comfortable disinfecting my hands. Maybe splash on some whisky, too, if they have any."

"Can I come?" said Koto, sliding off the top bunk.

"Sure. And I wanna see if I can get my own cabin."

"Me too."

They hurriedly left and slammed the door. *Bang!*

Nakayama brooded. The ship churned unctuously through the waves.

Finally, he said to no one in particular, "As if *she*, a woman who *boxes*, was marriageable to begin with!"

✳

Nagasaki. November 1906.

"Sen-*chan*! The mailman came!" called his mother.

She had been horrified when she heard of the stab wound from his Singapore trip. Although the wound was healing properly, her son insisted on weekly medical check-ups, claiming that the tropics were full of "unknown viruses". His letters were so incoherent that she decided to move from the country back to their Nagasaki townhouse to watch over him.

Nakayama came thumping down the stairs. He picked up the letter from his father and thumped back up, two steps at a time, to read it in the privacy of his study.

"Is it a work letter or family letter, my dear?" she called after him.

"Work letter. Father already wrote a family letter last week!"

"Sometimes he writes two family letters in a row. I was hopeful!"

She made a pot of tea.

"Mother?" his voice came floating down.

"Hm?"

"If you find another man you'd like to marry, dump Father. I won't object."

"Ha ha ha!"

"It's not too late. Carpe diem, Mother."

"I'll remarry when you get married, how's that?"

"You'll to wait till I'm FORTY."

She sat down at the lace-covered dining table for afternoon tea. "I've received more photos from the matchmaker! Come down and see them!"

"Kekkō desu." (No thanks.)

Nakayama worked on transcribing his father's letter. Progress was slow as he had to re-write it, word by word. His father's correspondence was always encoded. His pencil travelled across his letter pad, carefully converting strokes into other strokes. Just when he got used to a code, his father would switch to a new one. The "family letters" were the same way, except the code was different. His mother was in charge of those. She was much faster at figuring out every new code, a skill that often made him wonder at why she insisted on being a simple housewife. Reading each precious missive from Nakayama Masayoshi was, for both mother and son, a labor of love.

At last he was done. With a sigh, Nakayama sat back and read the sentences that he had revealed.

...Surround yourself with the best people and trust them.

Hold on to a sense of outrage.

Above all, marry the right person. I have never been more sure about anything in my life than my decision to marry your mother. As a consequence, I have never had any doubts about you.

What does it mean to become Oguri?

What does it mean to destroy him?

Only you can find out.

He lit a match and put paper to fire.

From the house across the street, directly below his study window, came the familiar sound of piano played by small, hesitant hands. There was nothing in the world that was more wretchedly middle-class than that sound. Why had he not thought so before? Japan, clean and gleaming as a teacup in a china cabinet.

Downstairs, his mother carefully slit open a thick envelope of photos with a letter opener. She laid each photo respectfully on the tablecloth. "Wow. There's a girl who speaks English. Right here in Nagasaki."

"There are plenty of girls who speak English in Nagasaki."

"Not *Japanese* girls." She paused, hoping for further remarks from her son. There were none. She sighed and turned that photo face down. She continued, addressing the ceiling, "Here's a very pretty girl from Tokyo who has published her first novel." As there was no response, she talked to herself. "Hm. Doesn't say what kind of novel it was. I suppose that's important. What if she writes *crime* novels? That wouldn't do. Talking to her would be like talking about work for Sen-*chan*." She poured herself another cup of tea and perused more photographs and introduction letters. "Sen-*chan*, what about a girl from Akita? You don't meet people from Akita every day. She hunts bears. For recreation. How interesting. She's willing to move to Nagasaki because the menfolk in Akita don't allow her to hunt in their mountains. Because it's considered bad luck to see a woman when a man is out on a hunt. Because..." she read on. "Because the Goddess of the Mountain would be jealous and not yield to the men her animal assets! Have you ever! How idiotic. Why, I feel like writing her to tell her to come down to Nagasaki anyway, whether she marries my son or not. She simply must get away from such Neanderthals."

"There...are...no...bears...in...Nagasaki..." sang her son from upstairs.

"Speaking of hunting girls, that boxing girl, that American, she was very interesting. Would I see her again?"

"No."

"Has she left for America?"

"No. I've sent her away on a secret mission for me."

"Goodness, is she in your employ?"

"Yes."

"Oh," she was disappointed. "She's only a work friend then? You have Americans working for you now?"

"I have all sorts." He came thumping down the stairs again and rang for the maid. "Have this letter delivered immediately. It goes to Father. Thanks!"

"Yes, *botchan*." The maid skipped off, glad for the errand.

His mother asked, "Has Koto-*kun* returned from Amakusa?"

"Not yet. He wrote that he'll be back in time for Christmas. He's Catholic. He wants to do Christmas Mass with me and Sparrow here. At Oura Cathedral. He's never been. I promised to take him."

"Oh." She wore a face of pretend respect. She was, after all, firmly Shinto and Buddhist, although she believed other religions 'interesting'. "Christmas Mass, huh."

"It'll be my first," said Nakayama, sitting down and cutting himself a slice of *castella* cake.

"You're welcome to come. You'll see Sparrow then, if you're such a big fan of hers."

"Are you truly and wholly Catholic now?"

"I told you, I got baptized the moment I got back."

"Who is the pastor? I can explain to him that you now regret. You were in a panic, you thought you were really ill."

"The process is quite irreversible," he assured her. "Anyway, I was looking into it before I left."

"But you said the cross on the wall was for vampires!"

"It's dual purpose."

She glared at him. Then, she said sternly, "Not a word of this to your grandparents."

"Yes Ma'am."

"Darjeeling tea?" She poured.

"Thank you."

"Sen-*chan's* not going through his tea as quickly as usual. I used to have to bring a new tin quite regularly!"

"Yes, I seem to have lost the taste for it." He noticed her expression and lied, "Everyone at the office drinks coffee."

"What a shame. Oh, speaking of office...what's the latest with Koto-*kun's* sister news?"

"I forgot to tell you. He's found out that he's had more than one older sister."

"Oh my goodness!"

"One was sold by her brothel owner to some tin mine up north. Federated Malay States. We don't know where. That's what happens when the girls are too old or too sick to work in Singapore: they're sold off to mines."

She was incredulous. "They work in *mines?*"

"No, they service the men who work in mines." He darted a look at his mother's stricken expression. "She's impossible to track. Those mining towns are..." He shook his head. "She's probably no longer alive, but Koto won't give up. Another sister was traced to the Japanese cemetery in Singapore. A mass grave. No individual names, but all Japanese prostitutes are buried there. She is most likely there. The third is still living. She's the one that he's visiting right now, in Amakusa. I don't know how she managed to return: you'd have to ask him when he comes. A total of three older sisters. All different fathers. Oh, and he found out about *his* father. From the living sister, the one in Amakusa. He was a policeman, of all things. From Beijing. No idea what he was doing in Singapore back then. That's all his sister knew. She didn't know his name. She was a child then, she just called him 'Beijing Uncle'. She said Koto looks like him. That's it. That's all he's got to go on."

"Poor Koto-*kun.*" His mother grew quiet for a while. Then she blinked and said lightly, "A northern Chinese father! That explains his height. Northerners are always tall."

"Nonsense. You and Father are tall. Only I am short."

"Well," she replied with a little smile. "All the growth went to your brain cells."

"Thank you, Mother."

"You're welcome, son." But the air in the dining room had changed; their usual banter did nothing to dissipate it.

"Is this cake from my favorite shop?"

"Yes it is. Why don't you finish it. Where are you going?"

"To the canal." Nakayama took the entire cake stand with him.

"Have you taken up smoking?" she called after him worriedly. That was the only explanation she could think of for his daily outdoor absences.

"Helps with the work stress," he said, and disappeared down the lane.

✳

"How can you do this?" he had shouted angrily at Plum.

He had opened a door on the top floor of The Blue Poppy Laundry Shop and seen a roomful of little girls sitting on shabby cotton mats. Waiting for customers. "They're *tiny*!"

"It's not *me* who's doing anything," she had said. She blew out a cloud of smoke. "It's *them*. Blame *their* parents. Look, when people are poor, they sell their children. This is true in every country. Not just Japan. You want to blame something, blame Poverty. Yes, Poverty. There are more people alive in this world than there should be." She offered him her pipe. "Think of a herd of deer. You can't pity the ones that are caught by the lion. Everyone is born with life. Everyone has an equal chance. Some are eaten. That's all."

✳

Kek-kek-kek went his wooden clogs on the flagstones.

Down, down the hill slope with the marvelous view of the crinkly sea and the flags stiff in the wind; past the neighbor's immaculate Japanese garden and its little bamboo pipe fountain; then a right turn to the crumbly, slightly damp path through the wild grasses, which led to the burbling canal with shallow steps in it that created miniature cascades. It carried rainwater, tadpoles, the odd duck into the sea. It was only a man-made canal of granite blocks, but when he closed his eyes he could almost believe he was once again by the dimpled brook of his childhood home in England.

Kanpeki.

He froze. A little girl in a bright red kimono was occupying the spot. *His* spot: the steps, half-hidden by wisteria bushes, next to the canal.

"Hello," she said.

He realized it was only his neighbor's daughter. The piano player.

He demanded, "What are you doing here?"

"Hiding."

"From who?"

"My mother."

"Why?"

"She wants me to take cod liver oil." Her eyes brimmed with tears. "After that she wants me to continue practicing piano." She began to sob quietly. "She is so mean."

Hnhp...hnhp!...hnhp! That slow, little hiccupy crying, partially suppressed. Sometimes their mouths opened but no sound came out. That was the worst of all. He had nightmares about that sound. He wished desperately she would stop. He offered her his handkerchief. She shook her head miserably.

"My life...is a d-disaster!" She blew her nose on her sleeve. "I shall kill myself."

"Don't be silly," he said abruptly. "No one kills themselves over a fate of cod liver oil and Mozart. Can I sit?"

"*Dozo,*" she whimpered.

He offered the cake stand in his hand. "Want some *castella?*"

"No thanks. I'm not allowed to eat sweets. Mother doesn't want me to get f-fat." She dried her eyes.

He thought it the perfect time to discuss a matter that had been bothering him for a very long time. "*Ne, ojōsan,*" he began. "*Ne...*Mozart...do you like his work?"

She sniffed, staring at the canal. She shook her head bitterly.

He warmed up to her. "*Sou ka...*I was wondering...have you heard of Ernest Hogan?"

She shook her head.

"Ragtime?"

She shook her head.

"I can teach you. I visited America last year. I came across a very new sound, very unforgettable. See, to me, it's madness that children don't play ragtime, it's so fun..."

She swung her head around, startled. Up the slope, a woman appeared, clutching a brown glass bottle and a spoon. The little girl gasped and dashed off in the other direction. The wisteria bush quivered.

Nakayama sighed. A complete defeat. But at least the spot had been returned to him.

It smelled of early November.

For more than two weeks he had not had normal air – not in ships, not in the humid, oppressive wrap of Singapore. He did not even notice what he lacked until his return. His body had adapted.

Up the hill, in the neighbor's garden, water trickled into a bamboo tube until it filled up more – more – until it was full – then tipped itself, dumped out its water, and swung back in place: *TUK-kuk*.

What an empty, pointless sound!

TUK-kuk.

The bamboo tube filled with water again. Why?

✳

"It is a type of *shishi odoshi* 鹿威し, Sen-*chan*," said his mother when they first moved back to Japan. He had never heard the sound before. "To intimidate deer. Otherwise the deer will eat all the flowers."

"But there are no deer in the city."

"True. Now people use the bamboo *sōzu* 添 水 for decoration. They like the sound."

"Like it! That eternal *tuk-tukking* drives me mad!"

"You must be a deer, Sen-*chan*. Just as I always thought."

✳

Nakayama Sen finished eating his cake. He flung the last of the crumbs at a nearby duck. Then he reached into his silk kimono jacket and untied two deerskin items from his cloth belt. The small leather sheath held his bamboo-stemmed tobacco pipe, tipped at both ends with brass. The round drawstring pouch held the tobacco. He pulled the fine, hair-like strands and stuffed them into the small bowl.

TUK-kuk.

He wasn't addicted, he told himself, lighting a match. The tobacco was just steeped in it, then dried. The amount in question was negligible. If he was ever discovered buying it, he would say it was medicine prescribed for his pain. Anyway he only smoked a few times a day. It required the greatest self-discipline not to do more. He checked his watch. He was careful to spend not more than half an hour, or his mother would come looking for him. He was glad she was there.

TUK-kuk, said the bamboo in reply.

He thought of the contents of the latest letter from his father. Could he pull it off?

He thought of Koto. It was a beautiful autumn day. Was he out sailing on his new fishing boat with his sister?

He blew out smoke. The lone duck swam about the canal, propelled by invisibly busy legs. It made no noise at all. The piano player was still on the run. It was the dead part of the afternoon.

TUK-kuk. The softest note in the universe, but once you noticed it you would start anticipating the next one, even if you dreaded it. He wished for the caw of a crow, the bark of a dog, even the slam of a gate. Nothing stirred.

The next *TUK-kuk* would come right...about...now...

"Botchan," he said out loud to himself, just to break the pattern. *"Dō suru?"*

The question hung in the sunshine.

He wondered if Sparrow was safe. Was it a mistake to send her there? But if anyone could do it, it would be her.

Just last week, he had stood in this very same spot with her.

"They know, *botchan*," she had said. "Of course the girls and their families know what they're getting into. Oguri's been shipping Shimabara and Amakusa girls into Singapore for decades. The girls send money home."

"But they were illiterate. Even if they wrote they never told the truth," he had replied.

The wind buffeted her hair that day. She turned to him and said, a strange expression on her face. "When they die they ask others to send home their portraits. The photos. Of them dressed like that. How could their families not know?"

"No. I have evidence that they were lied to; kidnapped."

"The truth is somewhere in between. They were told they would get good money. That's enough for them. That's why it has gone on. All I'm saying is, stopping it at its source might be harder than you think." She shook her head. "You and Koto are just two stupid Christian boys. You can't even save yourselves."

He shouted after her. "Where are you going?"

"I've got work to do." She held up a hand in farewell. "And be careful with your medicine, *botchan*. I've seen what it can do."

She never returned his name seal. He had to order a new one. She did, however, made him the present of a brand new watch chain of pure gold. He reached into his clothes to make sure it was still there.

It hurt a little, always, to think of Sparrow. Today he shall not think of Sparrow.

There was so much else to think of.

NAGASAKI – SHANGHAI – HONG KONG – SINGAPORE - MANILA – SAN FRANCISCO

TUK-kuk. Faint, but unmistakable.

"Jizo-san, Jizo-san," he began to sing. Just to drown out the *sōzu.* It was a song he had learned in Singapore. He sang slowly, trying to recall the words:

Jizo-san, Jizo-san

What are you doing on Flower Street?
Who are you protecting?
Hey, hey, look here, there's a Jizo statue
Give him a pebble or two

Jizo-san, Jizo-san
What are you doing on Flower Street?
This is not a town for children
Hey, hey, look here, there's a Jizo statue
Give him a bib, a pinwheel

In summer I'll give you rice cakes
In winter I'll knit you a coat
But I don't understand, I think you're lost
For there are no children here

He went to the canal and inverted the bowl of his pipe. With a sharp knock against the railings, he sent the ashes fluttering into the water, then he carefully slid the pipe back in its case. He took a deep breath, leaned back, shut his eyes, and listened to the endless wet murmuring of the canal.

TUK-kuk.

FIN

End Notes

メイキング

Books are like soufflés: you never know how they'd turn out.

Sometimes you measure everything perfectly, and cook them at the exact temperature and for the right amount of time, but they still fail to rise. On other occasions, you don't do much, but when you come back to check on them, they've risen into a giant, golden puffy mound in half the time you had expected. Because you never know how they'd turn out, it's best to be writing several books at once!

Kami + Kaze was a good soufflé. In the back of that book, I wrote that the story came to me in a flash after I read a single, critical sentence in a history textbook. I began writing and it turned out the way I liked.

In the case of *The Great Impresario Oguri*, I was inspired by an arresting Edwardian photograph of a Japanese pimp in Western coattails and top hat.

It was so extraordinary that I immediately sat down and wrote this tale. Characters like Sparrow, Nakayama, Koto came tumbling into my mind; memories of visiting early 20th century steamship museums in Japan; even songs, jaunty little tunes by the cultural icon Misora Hibari 美空ひばり, who didn't come along till the 1940s, somehow found themselves littering the pages of this book. I wrote quickly because I couldn't wait to sit down and consume it myself, which is the main reason why I write (and bake soufflés).

A Japanese soufflé from Hoshino Coffee Shops found (only) in Japan & Singapore

The pimp photo appeared in Professor James Francis Warren's famous ***Ah Ku and Karayuki-san: Prostitution in Singapore, 1870-1940***

(Oxford University Press, 1993). According to Warren, the man in the photo was the *zegen* Muraoka Iheiji. In the photograph, the *zegen* was a youthful-looking 41. It was taken in 1908 in Manila. He is shown posing rather ostentatiously with what looked like a watch drawn from a chain from his vest pocket. He had a bit of a Ringling Brothers air about him, but make no mistake: he controlled a sinister enterprise that trafficked in women. The scene of Nakayama at the piers at night, talking to the ship chandler, and the chilling contents of the handkerchief, was inspired by a line from Warren's book.

Warren, in his Preface, said that he "wanted to write a history of the Chinese and Japanese women in Singapore full of imaginative drama and narrative sweep". He succeeded. Relying on primary accounts, many by the prostitutes themselves, Warren has reconstructed a compassionate and richly-detailed story about colonial Singapore. It is a vision of my home country that I believe has never before appeared in any movie, television drama, or novel, let alone school textbook.

In comparison to Warren's thick and fascinating tome, *The Great Impresario Oguri* is but a short, fictional caper: it purports to be neither history nor fact. I've taken many liberties. For example, there was no way **Dr. Sun Yat-sen** 孫中山 would have met the Nakayamas in London during that particular time period, for he was still a teenager. I have also made liberal use of comedy and what my critics have labeled as 'banter'. Apparently lightheartedness is never allowed when tackling serious subjects, but I have been too infected, from an early age, by Evelyn Waugh to turn back at this point. Anyway, who wants a heavy story? We already know Life sucks. Surely there must be some other way to draw readers into an important and timely subject without producing yet another thick, fat novel showcasing the 'scar-misery' of Asia.

Now, what is true in this tale?

Karayuki-san 唐行さん really existed, and after you read Professor Warren's book, you can watch moving interviews with real-life *karayuki-san* in Shohei Imamura's 今村昌平 excellent film *Karayuki-san: The Making of a Prostitute* (1975), which I found online. It's not depressing, and it will change your view of the relationship between Southeast Asia and Japan forever. Imamura has made the study of strong Japanese women in the margins of society his favorite subject. You might want to watch more of his films if you like this kind of thing.

The story of how Koto was given away at the hospital, and how his birth mother almost changed her mind, came from real-life conversations I had with Chinese women who remembered a time before contraception was affordable or even available in Singapore. Everybody back then was always adopting or giving away babies. Or they'd swap babies to get the gender they wanted. My ancestry, once traced, is wonderfully chaotic as a result.

For a great commentary on this practice, watch Studio Ghibli's *From Up Poppy Hill* コクリク坂 から. Based on a manga by Sayama Tetsuro 佐山哲郎 and Takahashi Chizuru 高橋千鶴, it is set in postwar Yokohama, one of my favorite nautical cities. American film critics (who had no business watching sophisticated anime) dismissed the child-swapping plot as cheap melodrama. Asian audiences would instantly recognize it as heartbreaking, if mundane, truth. Don't miss how **Kyu Sakamoto's** 1961 hit *Sukiyaki* is used in that film. Kyu ('nine') was the last of nine kids – I always thought it was lucky he wasn't given away!

Nagasaki 長崎市 was very cosmopolitan, with many imported things such as Catholicism and Portuguese pound cake (*castella*), before it involuntarily acquired world status as the tragic site of American atomic bombing. I chose to portray this old Nagasaki to remind everyone not to always see cities in their current freeze-frame. It is not fair to the city or its people. You can read Swiss professor (from UCLA) Herbert E. Plutschow's **Old Nagasaki** for inspiration before you visit.

The photo on the front book cover is of the **Hikawa Maru** 氷川丸 which is permanently parked in Yokohama harbor. You can go inside to see what a Japanese 'Titanic' looked like from that era. Unlike the Hollywood version, in real-life everything on board a luxury liner is very small in scale. I remember reading that the Third Class passengers were very close to the ship's crew, because they were from the same social strata, and often helped them out on the voyage by doing odd jobs on the ship. Visiting the First versus Third Class cabins, I realized that First Class was just a hotel, no different from those on land; Third Class, in contrast, was a village. No doubt Third had more fun at sea. Koto's description of travelling in Cargo came from my elderly relatives' accounts of their voyages in the

1940s. They were too poor to even afford Third. They just found a space to sit among the goods in the Cargo hold and toughed it out. I'm not sure if it was even legal to keep humans in there, but ships' captains were certainly not above people-smuggling as it was extremely profitable. I read that steamships, whether in Asia or in the West, were often overcapacity by a few hundred passengers, without being discovered.

I was astonished, when I moved to America, that most Americans have not heard of **carrom,** a game the men in my Singapore family played when I was little. I had assumed, like most board games, that it came from the West, but it actually is from the Indian subcontinent. It is analogous to billiards, but simpler and cheaper, without cue sticks. The board is set directly on the floor. I grew up with that unmistakably loud sound. The adult players would shake talcum powder on the board to enable the counters to slide smoothly, an essential feature of the game that instantly attracted anyone under the age of two. Carrom is still played today in Singapore.

Saint Anthony's Convent in Singapore really existed; in fact it is now Saint Anthony's Canossian Secondary School and still only accepts girls. It was Mrs Monica Menon from its excellent English Literature Department who invited me to meet their literature teachers in 2016. I was delighted to find that these men and women came from all races and religions. One was a Chinese nun. They gave me a publication of the school's history, which dated back to 1879. I'll never forget the sepia photographs showing barn-like wooden schools in the tropical heat, with European nuns teaching dozens of scraggly Chinese and Indian girls how to read and write. Some of these kids were orphans, but many were simply abandoned by indigent parents because they were female. I showed these photographs to other Singaporeans and foreign expatriate friends living in Singapore, who exclaimed that they had never seen "this Singapore". Me neither.

It's easy to believe the **Singapore** of Marina Bay Sands (three modern megaliths stabbing the sky, F-1 night race track, &c.) had always existed, but Singapore was a far more interesting and diverse place before, like so many modern cities in Europe and Asia, it became irreversibly changed by the Second World War and what happened after. You can find on YouTube, for example, a 1938 British Pathe film showing how built-up and modern Singapore already was at the time. It was a true, cosmopolitan city rivaling Shanghai in architectural appearance. Few of these structures remain.

The Singapore neighborhoods that housed a colorful Japanese community before WWII have long been demolished. Growing up in 1980s Singapore, I probably speak for many Singaporeans when I say that we had two views of Japan: first, the bright and shiny Japan which gave us Hello Kitty, J-Pop, and the ubiquitous Sony Walkman. Second, the Japan which ruthlessly bombed, shot, and raped us during WWII. I only recently learned, first-hand from relatives who survived the war, that many of those 'Japanese' soldiers were in fact Taiwanese of the same Chinese ethnicity as ourselves who were recruited from Japan's colony. That troubling bit of ambiguity was always left out in the history books and movies.

In writing this book, and many others, I have tried to portray not just the black and the white, but the grey. I will never forget or forgive what Japan did to Singapore, for it directly affected members of my family. My relatives still mourn those who died and the architecture which was burned to the ground by Japanese bombing. In their dreams, they still walk the shops and visit the homes whose interiors they remember so vividly. There are family stories that I have not set down on paper: truth can be so pathetically sad and personal that the novelist must draw a line. The only thing I can do to stop myself from hating an entire race of people for the rest of my life is remind myself of the suffering of ordinary Japanese civilians, particularly women, when a country is hell-bent on, as historians call it, "entering the Dark Valley". Somewhere in Japan, the elderly counterparts of my Chinese relatives, too, are dreaming of siblings, friends, and the interiors of homes that have been erased by Allied bombs.

In Singapore today, some of the streets which once housed Japanese brothels and businesses are now encased by an air-conditioned mall, **Bugis Junction**. When I was little, I used to play inside **Shaw Towers**, where my father worked – an office building built on the ghostly remains of the red-light district where Nakayama, Plum, Koto and his rickshaw driver traversed in this book. A guest used to be able to just exit **Raffles Hotel** and stroll over to the Japanese brothels of Hylam Street.

All ghosts, however, are not buried. As I write, North Korea has just bragged of its largest nuclear test: a bomb seven times the size of what the US dropped on Hiroshima.

Singapore is still a bustling port located in Southeast Asia, a region in which little girls, not to mention women, are still sold for sex. Volunteer organizations like **ECPAT (End Child Prostitution & Trafficking)** have toiled for decades to redress this wrong. The scene where Nakayama stumbles into a room full of children sitting on mats is taken directly from a friend's account. When he heard I was writing this book, he told me of what he had personally encountered in the recent past, on a beach in a Southeast Asian country. Sitting in rusty shipping containers, which served as 'hotels', were little bedraggled girls of ten or twelve, waiting for customers. Nakayama's shout to Plum upon the shock of discovery, "How can you do this! They're tiny!" were in fact my friend's, uttered on that occasion. The native tour guide who had taken him there had replied in Plum's exact words regarding poverty – words so simple and damning that I saw no reason to embellish further.

Today, the main patrons of these lonely outposts of affordable sex are rumored to be middle-aged Chinese taxi drivers from Singapore. A century ago, it was Singapore's rickshaw drivers, such as the one who ferried Koto to Hylam Street, who needed cheap sex. Some things never change. As for Western sailors who disembark at Singapore looking for action, an American friend of mine who was ex-Navy, upon hearing where I grew up, told me that being taken by a trishaw (Singapore's current iteration of the rickshaw) to the red-light district was the first thing he and his sailor pals did when they docked. This was in the 1990s. No doubt this still goes on today. No offense was meant to me by my friend in sharing that anecdote, and none was taken. Yet deep down inside me, there is a little voice that whispers, "Some Are Eaten."

After reading this book, I hope you will keep your eyes peeled for any modern day Sayuris, Hinas, and Kotos lurking in Singapore's glittering casino-and-café world. Even if we can't personally find and help each one of them, the least we can do is acknowledge their suffering by telling their story. And if you ever see an Oguri, I hope you draw inspiration from the courage of the three friends in this book.

This book is for Madam Xie 謝亞美. With Chinese storytellers like her around, the novelist's work is easy.

Wena Poon

Austin, Texas
August 2017

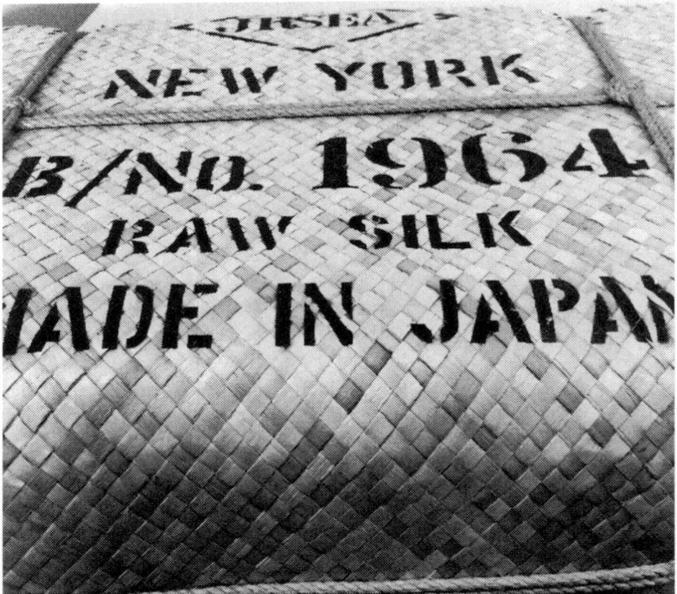
NEW YORK
B/NO. 1964
RAW SILK
ADE IN JAPA

BOXING

KUMO'S PUB NAGASAKI (NEAR DOCKYARD)

SEE

ALICE "SPARROW"

TAKE ON THE

"MAN OF KLANG"

DOORS OPEN AT 6 O'CLOCK SHARP

BRING YOUR OWN CIGARS

LIGHT SUPPER, WINES & SPIRITS AVAILABLE

ADMISSION FREE

Books By the Same Author

- NOVELS -
The Biophilia Omnibus (2009)
Alex y Robert (2010)
Novillera (2013)*
Kami + Kaze (2014)*
Café Jause (2014)*
Chang'an (2016)
Shonanto no Ramen (2016)*
The Adventures of Snow Fox & Sword Girl (2014)*
Voyage to the Dark Kirin (2015)*
The Marquis of Disobedience (2016)*
The Great Impresario Oguri (2017)

- SHORT FICTION -
Lions in Winter (2007)
The Proper Care of Foxes (2009)
Maxine, Aoki, Beto & Me (2013)*

- NON-FICTION -
On Making Madeleines (2016)

featuring original photography

All books available worldwide on Amazon, eBay, Book
Depository, and other US and international online retailers.
Also at select bookstores, libraries and universities.
More information at www.wenapoon.com

スタジオウェナ

About The Author

WENA POON's novels and short stories have been professionally produced on the London stage, serialized as a *Book At Bedtime* on BBC Radio 4, and extensively anthologized and translated into French, Italian, and Chinese. She won the UK's Willesden Herald Prize for best short fiction. She was also nominated for Ireland's Frank O'Connor Award, France's *Prix Hemingway*, the Singapore Literature Prize, and the UK's Bridport Prize for Poetry. Her fiction is studied by British, American, Hong Kong and Singapore academics as examples of transnational literature. From 2011 through 2017, her short stories are studied by thousands of Singapore high school students sitting for the Cambridge 'O' Level Exams in Literature. She graduated *magna cum laude* in English Literature from Harvard and holds a J.D. from Harvard Law School. She speaks English, Mandarin and French and is an international lawyer by profession. Her Web site is www.wenapoon.com.

Thank you for reading!

じゃ、またね～

スパロ：一番最強！ (Sparrow is Number 1!)